Another Sad Love Song

Also by
La Jill Hunt

Drama Queen
No More Drama

Shoulda, Woulda, Coulda

Anthology:

Around the Way Girls
Around the Way Girls 2
A Dollar and a Dream

Another Sad Love Song

La Jill Hunt

URBAN BOOKS LLC

Urban Books LLC
10 Brennan Place
Deer Park, NY 11729

ISBN: 978-0-7394-7347-4

Printed in the United States of America

*This is a work of fiction. Any references or similarities to actual
events, real people, living, or dead, or to real locales are intended
to give the novel a sense of reality. Any similarity in other names,
characters, places, and incidents is entirely coincidental.*

Acknowledgments

To God, for once again, giving me the opportunity to utilize the talents you bestowed upon me.
To my family, for constant love and encouragement.
To my daughters, for inspiring and providing comic relief when Mommy needs it. I love you!
To Pastor Brown and the Mt. Lebanon Missionary Baptist Church family, thanks for your continual love and support.
To Carl and Martha Weber, for all you do.
To Roy Glenn, Dwayne S. Joseph and K. Elliott, my big brothers who are always there.
To Arvita Glenn for accepting my 50 million excuses!!
To Milly Avent, Omeida Cutler, Toye Farrar and Selena Johnson, thanks for always reading when I need you to!!!
To all the readers who support me and my dream—
I appreciate you more than you'll ever know!!

Feel free to email me at *MsLajaka@AOL.com*

Be on the lookout: Coming November, 2006
Too Close For Comfort

Another Sad Love Song

Prologue

"Mo Money Mo Problems"

—Notorious B.I.G.

I couldn't help smiling as I pulled out of the parking lot. There was no doubt in my mind that the job I had just interviewed for was mine. It was my second and final interview with the telephone company, and I know I dazzled them. Before I even entered the office to meet with the managers who I had been informed I needed to see, I knew I had the job. I could feel it. I was well-educated, having received my MBA last spring. My résumé was impressive; my letters of recommendation praised my outgoing personality, team-player attitude, and impeccable work record. I was a hard worker and knew that I deserved this job. It was mine. There was no reason for me not to have it.

Even though I was feeling positive, I said a quick prayer, asking God to look out for me because this was the opportunity I had worked for. I popped in my *Life After Death* CD and turned the volume up, bobbing my head to the beat of the music. I was feeling so good that I was tempted to drop the top on my car.

It was still early on a Wednesday afternoon, and I thought about what I could do to kill some time. I decided to ride across town to my best friend Dorian's car lot and see what he was up to. Pulling into the left lane, I stopped at the red light and waited for the signal to give me the go-ahead to turn. I sat for a few minutes and watched the light, singing along with the music. When the green arrow flashed, I let off the brakes and hit the gas as I turned the steering wheel.

I caught a glance of a car coming toward me, but I didn't pay it any attention, confident that I clearly had the right of way. With the music blasting, there was no way I could hear the screeching of tires or the blaring of a horn, but I did feel the impact of the Toyota Camry hitting the front left side of my car. I slammed on the brakes and immediately stopped. For some reason, my first instinct was to turn down the radio as the reality of what had just happened slowly sank in.

My baby. I unhooked my seatbelt and opened my door. My sleek, black Mercedes 280 was the closest thing I had to having a child and my most prized possession. Especially since it was a graduation gift and I didn't have to pay a dime for it. There was no way that someone could have been stupid enough to hit my baby. *This can't be happening.*

I stepped outside the vehicle and saw that the front left side was a crumpled, mangled mess. There was a hissing sound coming from somewhere. I didn't know if it was from my engine or the car that had so viciously slammed into me. I shook my head in disgust, feeling both anger and frustration at the same time.

My eyes traveled to the white Toyota Camry that was the source of the chaos. The hood was smashed in so bad, I couldn't even see the driver. *Probably some old woman whose cataracts are so bad, she can't even see the damn light.* I could feel my stress level rising as I waited for her to get out.

"Hey, are you all right?" A guy called out from a pickup truck behind the Camry.

"Yeah, I'm good." I reached for my cell phone, which was attached to my belt.

"She just plowed right into you, man. I saw her run the light. She was too busy yapping on the cell phone to see anything. I'm a witness; I saw the entire thing. It was her fault." The guy walked over toward me.

"Yeah."

"Okay, I called 911 already, and they're on their way." He nodded.

"Thanks." I placed my cell back into its holder.

The driver of the Camry still hadn't emerged. I walked closer and saw that the airbag had deployed. I had been so caught up in the damage to my car that I disregarded the fact that someone could've very well been hurt.

Just as I was reaching to open the door to the car, it flung open. I was surprised when it wasn't a 90-year-old woman wearing a wig and a housecoat who emerged, but a young woman who happened to be so striking that, for a moment, I forgot all about the accident.

"Oh my God! Oh my God! I can't believe this," she cried out as she walked to see the damage.

"Jesus, what am I gonna do? Oh, Lord, this is not happening . . . not now . . . please not now!"

"Ma'am, are you okay?" I asked her. Now that I saw that she was okay, I dialed 911 as I watched her pace back and forth, her hands holding her head.

"I can't deal with this, not today!" She continued talking to herself.

"Man, I think she's in shock or something," Mr. Pickup Truck told me.

"Miss, I think you should calm down," I suggested; "it's going to be all right."

"No, it's *not* going to be all right." She shook her head and cried, "Why me? I've been driving since I was 16 years old. Sixteen! Never had an accident in my life, and today of all days, I run into a damn Benz! My luck can't get any worse."

Cars began going around us and I ignored the rubberneckers stretching to see what happened. I know that if we didn't hurry and get out of the road soon, we would cause a traffic buildup for miles.

She leaned over and began heaving.

I didn't know if she was about to throw up or what. I walked a little closer and could see that she was gasping for air. "Maybe you should sit down for a minute," I told her. "The police are on their way, and everything is gonna be fine." I tried to give her a smile to assure her it was going to be all right.

She shook her head again and closed her eyes, still gasping for air.

Again, I took a step closer to her. Even in the midst of all the chaos, I couldn't help noticing she had the most perfect skin I had ever seen. *This girl is banging.* I tried not to think it, but there was no denying—she was a true beauty. I fought the urge to reach over and touch her arm.

I could see the rise and fall of her chest with every breath she took. "Look, just calm down and breathe," I said, knowing that something wasn't right. I could hear sirens coming toward us, which made me feel a little better. "Just chill; it's only a car. That's what insurance is for."

She looked over at me, and our eyes met. "My insurance expired day before yesterday," she said, right before her body crumpled to the ground.

It was my turn to close my eyes and try to breathe. *Damn, damn, damn!*

Chapter 1

"Boys to Men"

—New Edition

The sound of the alarm startled me to the point where I felt as if my heart would jump out of my chest. Not because I was asleep, but because I forgot that it was set. Usually, there was no need, because my internal clock woke me every morning without fail by 6 a.m.; even on the weekends when I wanted to sleep in. But seeing that it was Monday and a brother was the newest finance manager for Bell Communications, it definitely would've been inappropriate for me to walk in late on my first day. I knew the job was mine.

Ring! Ring! Ring!

For the second time that morning, I almost had a heart attack. *It has to be Momma,* I thought. *Only she would call me this early.* And knowing today was going to be my first day at my new job, I knew she'd call. "Good morning."

"Good morning, Koby. Are you up yet?"

"Yes, I am already up."

"Did you get much sleep last night, or are you nervous?"

"I slept pretty well."

"Are you still sore from the accident?"

"I'm fine, Ma," I told her, even though my neck and back were a little stiff. "Where's Pop?"

"Him and your Uncle Theodore are already up and gone to play golf. You'd think they were entering the Masters Tournament next year."

I laughed. "Momma, why are you talking about Pop like that? You never know . . . since retiring, golf may be his thing."

"*Getting on my nerves* is more like his thing. I swear, if I didn't know any better, I'd suggest he get another job, but that would probably make him even worse."

My dad, recently retired from the Ford plant, found himself with a lot of extra time on his hands. My mother hadn't retired yet; she still had a love for teaching. She was also a women's counselor at the church. My parents had been married thirty-two years and counting and had two children, my much younger fifteen-year-old brother, Jaamell, and me.

In fact, Jaamell was their change-of-life baby. Not many 11th graders had a father that was retired. Jaamell got the world, to my dismay. I couldn't say much, though; I spoiled him just as much as they did.

"Now guess what your father and uncle have decided to do?"

"Start playing tennis?"

"No. Start their own detailing business."

"Well, Ma, that may be a good thing. You know

Pop can wash some cars . . . and Uncle Theodore too."

"And I know how your father can start something and leave it hanging. Remember the moving company and the janitorial service. Oh, and who can forget the carpet-cleaning business."

I was laughing so hard, tears began to roll down my cheek.

Even before he retired, Pop and Uncle Theodore were constantly coming up with these brilliant businesses that were supposedly guaranteed to make money. The problem was that, after about two months, either they would get tired or get mad at each other, so the businesses would fail before they even got off the ground.

"But all in all, Koby, your father is a good man, and I couldn't have asked the Lord for a better husband or father for you boys."

"You're right about that. You and Pop have always been there for all of us."

"And you are a good man too, Koby. We are so proud of you and your achievements. Now, go on and get ready for work. And remember, son, you're blessed and highly favored, and God has got your back—"

"Because I'm special." I finished the phrase that Momma had instilled in me since I was a baby.

"That's right, baby, and don't you forget it. I love you, and have a blessed day."

"I love you, too. Kiss Pop for me and tell Jaamell I said, 'What's up.'" I hung the phone up feeling as if I could conquer the world. My mother's love had a way of doing that to me, I guess.

As I showered and dressed for my big day, I

meditated on the thought that even with the accident and my car being totaled, it seemed that everything was working in my favor for the moment.

Arriving at work on my first day, I tried to calm the butterflies in my stomach. "You were born to do this," I told myself. "This is what you have worked for, and you've earned it." You would've thought the theme song from *Rocky* was playing in my head as I entered the tall glass building and said, "Good morning," to my new co-workers as we rode the elevator to our designated floors.

"Good morning, Mr. Jackson." The department secretary greeted me with a smile. "Ready for your first day?"

"If I'm not, then it's too late to back down now, Ms. Juanita."

"Coffee is in the break room if you need a boost to get you started," she informed me.

"No, thanks. I'm good."

"Well, Brenda and Timothy are waiting to show you around and fill you in."

"Great. I guess I'll check in with them right now. This way, right?"

"You got it. Just let me know if you need anything."

I entered the conference room to meet with my colleagues. The district manager had already introduced me to Brenda Dollar. The feisty, friendly woman made me feel welcome instantly, and I felt comfortable around her already.

"All right now, Mr. Jackson, you ready for the races?" she asked with a wide smile.

I grinned at her. "As ready as I'm ever gonna be."

"Well, take your mark, and while you are at it, let me introduce you to your fellow runner, Timothy Brown. Tim, this is JaKoby Jackson."

"Nice to meet you, man. I've heard a great deal about you. We're really glad to have you here in our ranks." Tim extended his hand and made me feel as if he really meant it.

"All good things, I hope?" I replied, shaking his hand.

"He didn't get them from me, so they must be all good," Brenda said.

"Don't take her seriously, JaKoby. If she hadn't made a smart comment, then you would really have something to worry about. Why do you think I'm glad to have you aboard? Before you got here, I was the only one she had to pick on."

We all laughed, and at that moment, I knew that I would enjoy working there. Brenda and Tim held a brief office meeting to introduce me to the rest of the staff, and I met with my own personal team members to discuss my expectations and to get to know them and their expectations of me.

The day went by fast, and the week went by even faster. Before I knew it, it was Friday, and it was almost time to go home. Tim and I were headed out the door when I looked across the parking lot and stopped dead in my tracks as I watched two women talking next to a gold sedan. I tried to get a closer look to see if it was her or if I was mistaken, but the women got into the car before I could really tell.

"What's wrong?" Tim asked.

"Uh, nothing. I thought I saw someone I knew."

I hadn't had any contact with the woman who'd hit my car the week before. Although I wanted to call and see if she was okay, I decided not to. About the only thing I knew about her was her name—Chryslin Matthews—and the fact that she *didn't* have any car insurance.

"Wow, is this your car?" Tim asked, admiring the sleek black Lexus truck Dorian had given me as a loaner.

"I wish. No, I had a car accident last week, so this one is a loaner."

"Man, when I had a loaner car after my accident, they gave me a Chevy Malibu."

"I guess it does help that my best friend owns the dealership." I laughed and opened my door.

"Yeah, it is good to have friends in high places." He laughed. "See you Monday."

"Have a good weekend," I told him. As I pulled out of the parking spot, I glanced around to see if I saw the gold sedan, but it was long gone.

Chapter 2

"On My Own"

—Patti LaBelle

After I arrived home, I realized I hadn't checked my voicemail in two days. My evenings consisted of coming home, changing, lifting a few weights, and doing a little reading. I'd shower, watch ESPN, and get ready for the next day. *So much for the life of a bachelor.* I sat on the sofa and hit the play button. The generic voice announced that I had a grand total of four messages.

Koby, it's me, J. Yo, me and some friends wanna go to a concert upstate at the end of the month, and since you don't have Rhea up your butt anymore, I thought you might want to take us—oh yeah . . . please. Let me know, bro. Peace.

That was from my little brother Jaamell. Although he was intelligent, athletic, and popular, he was also an all-around smart-ass.

Now why would he think I'd take him and his equally smart-ass friends and drive two hours upstate to a concert? He has lost his mind. I erased the message.

Hey, Koby. It's Momma. I hope everything is going well with your new job. Jaamell and his friends want to go to some concert on the 24th, but I have a conference that weekend. I told him you might be free to take them. Be blessed and call me when you get this message.

Enough said, I thought. *That's where the idea came from—Momma. She's lost her mind too.* I decided to save that message.

Yo, Koby, it's Dorian. Just calling to say what's up, man. Holla back, if you hanging out tonight. Peace.

That was my homeboy, Dorian. Married but still free enough to hang out, his wife, Jackie was the total package: beautiful, smart, and kind. Dorian knew he was blessed to have her by his side. Although he loved the club scene, he knew where home was and made sure everyone else knew too.

Dorian played football in the NFL for three years until an injury to his Achilles tendon ended his career. He now owned the most successful luxury car dealership in the state. He was still in excellent physical condition, and when it came to fashion style, he gave Puffy a run for his money.

I waited for the last message:

Koby, it's Rhea. I was just calling to see how your week went. I haven't talked to you in a while, but I hope you are enjoying your new job. Call me soon. Bye. Oh and, Koby, I love you.

I groaned at the thought of Rhea Davidson, my ex. *Don't do it, man.* My mind instantly set off alarms. *DO NOT CALL HER BACK!*

Rhea and I had gone through enough drama to make *The Young and the Restless* look like a PBS documentary. It seemed as though every time I had gotten her out of my system, she was back. *Not this time.* It was time to move past Rhea and all her drama once and for all. *Definitely erase that nonsense!*

After checking my messages, I changed and grabbed a soda out of the fridge. Clicking on the television, I tried to chill for a bit but couldn't get the thought of Chryslin Matthews out of my mind. Man, she was beautiful. The cocoa-brown skin, the long lashes that seemed to go on forever, her eyes were like pools that seemed to drink me in.

"Man, stop tripping!" I told myself out loud. "You don't even know the girl." I began to wonder if I should send her some flowers as a gesture of goodwill. *Now you really are tripping—she hit your car fool; you ain't hit hers!*

Picking up the phone, I dialed my mother's number.

"JaKoby Jackson, I know you are not just now calling me two days after I left you a message."

"Hello to you too, Mother. Yes, I am fine. Thanks for asking. Oh, the job is great."

"Cute, Koby, but this is even cuter . . ." I heard her place the phone down and yell, "Jaamell, Koby is on the phone, and not only is he taking you and your buddies to the show, he's letting you guys stay at his house for the weekend. He'll pick you all up Friday afternoon after work!"

I could hear Jaamell whooping it up in the background as Momma picked the phone back up.

"Good one, Momma. And what am I supposed to do with them for the entire weekend?"

"Show them what it means to be a successful black man, not one that has the NBA contract, but one that got the MBA on scholarship. It's called *giving back*, JaKoby!"

Ooh, she hit me below the belt with that one. "A'ight, Ma, for you I will."

"Not for me, Koby, for them and, more importantly, for yourself. Now, end of that discussion. So, do you like your new job, sweetie?"

"Yeah, really I do. You really prayed this one up for me."

"You claimed this one yourself, remember. Hold on. Here's your father."

"Koby, my boy! How's it going? Your momma told me you like your new job."

"Pops, the hardest working retiree I know. How's Uncle Theodore? You guys staying out of trouble? What scheme, I mean business idea have you guys come up with these days?"

"Boy, don't play with me. Just because you're a 'big wig' doesn't mean you're too big for me to beat your behind."

I had to laugh when he said that. My father had only hit me twice in my entire life; once for riding my skateboard through Uncle Theodore's living room, which had white carpet at the time, and the second time for telling my teacher I didn't complete my homework because my father's mother had died the night before. (She'd actually died the year before I was born.)

"I'm just playing, Pop. How is the golf game?"

"Still working on it. You ought to come out and play with Theodore and me sometime. You need to learn now that you're in corporate America. You know that's where the big deals are made—on the green, Koby, on the green."

"Well, Pop, I might take you up on that offer real soon. I gotta go, now. Tell Momma I'll try to make it to church on Sunday. Love you, Pop. Bye."

After hanging up with Pop, I dialed Dorian's number.

"You enjoying the truck? Rides nice, huh? I think you should go ahead and keep it."

"I don't think so."

"Why not? You got a new job making all that loot; it's time to splurge."

"Nope, not the kid," I told him. Dorian knew there was no way I could afford a damn-near forty-thousand-dollar SUV.

"Your cheap ass." He laughed. "Yo, Koby . . . dawg, you gon' be on time tonight or what?"

"Yeah, *D*. What time you want me to be at your house?—you're the one with a curfew."

"Man, I choose to have a curfew. I don't want to still be out there when the freaks come out; I want to be curled up with my boo. It makes me appreciate what I have at home."

"Whatever. Be ready by nine."

"Bet. See you when you get here. Oh, and Koby, stay out of my closet tonight, son."

"Dorian, don't play with me. You know I got some gear that you wish you had."

Dorian and I usually used Friday nights at the club as our own personal runway. It wasn't unusual for us to find that we'd both have on the same color or style. Once, when he came to pick me up, we had on the exact same shirt. I firmly believed that great minds think alike, but you know I had to go and change with a quickness.

*   *   *

Thoughts of Chryslin entered my head again as I stood to turn off the TV. The ringing of the phone quickly interrupted them. "Hello."

"Hello, Koby. How's it going?"

"Good, Rhea. What's up?" I felt my heart beat faster and tried to sound glad that she called. I wanted to keep the conversation light and friendly in order to avoid any attitude from her.

"Just checking on you. How's the job going?"

"Great. I really like it so far."

"That's good. I'm really happy for you, Koby."

"Thanks, Rhea. Hey, can I call you back? I am about to—"

"Go hang out with Dorian. I figured you would be; I wanted to catch you before you left. I guess you can call me later." She sounded disappointed.

"I will. Talk to you later, Rhea."

"Koby, I love you."

I hung up before she could say anymore, because I didn't wanna hear it.

I met Rhea one Friday night while I was still in grad school. Dorian and I were standing at the bar, when she and some of her girlfriends made their grand entrance into the club. It was one of those rare occasions when Jackie had come along to hang out with us. She had gone over to a table to speak to some friends of hers, so it looked as if Dorian and I were alone.

It was then that one of Rhea's girlfriends walked up to Dorian and gushed all over him about how she thought he was so fine and how much she admired him. She pulled her tight, spandex dress down even farther, to reveal her "barely-there" cleavage. "So . . . would you like to buy us a drink?" she asked, referring to Rhea and her other two diva friends.

"I don't think that would be a good idea," Dorian told her.

"Aw, come on, Mr. Silver. How about a round for us?—I know you can afford it."

"It's not about the money." He looked at me with a twinkle in his eye. I was used to women throwing themselves at Dorian all the time.

She frowned. "Well, what is it then?"

"Because," Jackie said, "the only drinks he'll be buying tonight are for his wife."

Dorian wrapped his arms around her full body.

"She's your wife? Oh, I mean . . . pleased to meet you." Ms. Diva said, clearly embarrassed.

"Come on, baby, that's my joint!" Dorian yelled, pulling Jackie to the dance floor. They began to jam to "Before I Let Go" by Maze, featuring Frankie Beverly.

I heard a voice come from behind me. "Sorry about my friend."

I turned and saw a gorgeous face with striking green eyes staring back at me. Dressed in a black halter top and low-cut jeans; the hoop she wore in her navel caught my attention—immediately. She wore her hair in a style similar to Halle Berry's, short and close, and it looked good. *Not many women can pull off Halle.*

"Hey, no problem. It happens all the time, believe it or not."

"I'm Rhea . . . Rhea Davidson." She smiled at me.

I smiled back at her. "JaKoby Jackson. Nice to meet you."

"So, where's *your* wife?—she's not gonna come creeping up behind me, is she?"

"Nope. I'm not married."

"Oh, well your girlfriend isn't lurking around the corner either, right?"

"No, I don't have a girlfriend either." I had to laugh.

"Then, in that case, how about a dance?"

"Okay," I said, and we made our way to the crowded dance floor.

"Oh, snap! Check out Koby!" Dorian called out when he spotted me.

"Now, Koby, don't sweat the clothes up!" Jackie laughed.

We all danced and laughed together until the DJ put on some slow cuts. I turned to leave the floor and felt a hand on my back.

"Wait, please," Rhea said. "I love this song."

Slow dancing with strangers wasn't something I usually did, because it made me feel uncomfortable, but there was something pleading in her face that made me put my arms around her and walk back to the center of the floor.

She put her head on my shoulder as Tyrese serenaded us with "Sweet Lady."

After the song ended, we returned over to the table where Dorian and Jackie were seated. "Hey, anybody down for some IHOP?" Dorian asked.

"Well, I didn't drive. I rode with my friends." Rhea looked towards "the diva patrol," who chose that moment to walk over to us.

"Rhea, we are ready to go," head diva announced.

"Hey, I can give you a ride home, if you want to roll with us," I said.

"It's not safe for you to just leave with strangers," head diva responded.

Rhea looked at her, then at me, deciding what to do.

"We're not gonna abduct and murder her, if that's what you are worried about; we just invited her to breakfast. Besides, isn't my *fine* husband someone you *admire* so much? You know he wouldn't do anything to hurt her."

"It's okay, Jenae. I'll be all right," Rhea assured her.

"Well, call as soon as you get home; I'll be waiting," The diva patrol departed, and we headed for the parking lot.

Rhea and I trailed Jackie's Lexus in the 5-year-old Bronco my parents had given me as a high-school graduation gift.

"So, you don't play professional football, huh?" Rhea looked out the window.

"Nope. What made you think that?"

She turned to look at me. "Well, you are built like a football player and you are dressed fly as hell, not to mention you are hanging out with Dorian Silver. I just thought you were one of his teammates or something."

"No. No pro ball for me. But thanks for the compliment."

We made small talk until we arrived at the restaurant.

"So what do you do?" she asked as we sat at the table with Dorian and Jackie.

"Well, right now I am in graduate school, but I work in HR for Circuit City at the corporate office."

"That's good."

"What do *you* do?" Jackie asked her.

"I'm a legal assistant for Michael Puryear of Sykes, Jones and Puryear."

"Wow," Dorian commented, "they are one of the fastest-growing minority firms. Impressive."

"Yes, Michael is one of the most sought-after defense attorneys on the East Coast. He keeps me very busy. I love it though."

"I thought you would've been a model. You look like a model and you're dressed fly as hell, not to mention you were hanging with some model-type chicks," I said to everyone's amusement.

Rhea and I exchanged numbers, when I took her home that morning. We talked on the phone quite often and began to date regularly. Soon, we had fallen into a routine. Time seemed to fly, between work, class, and Rhea calling to remind me, "We've got plans." Those plans usually included a social gathering involving the firm. It was at these functions that I made several business contacts,

which led to my interview with the telephone company.

I refused to let old memories of "Rhea and what
could have been" spoil my mood. After the week I
had, I was hype to hang with my boy.

I clicked on the stereo and changed to the disc I
wanted. I hit the track and proceeded to get ready
for the night. Sounds of my boy, Usher, filled my
townhouse. "That's right," I told myself; "I just
gotta be smart about it."

"What's up, pimp!" Dorian greeted me with a
grin, looking like the true player he wanted to por-
tray in all black, right down to the gator boots. The
two-carat studs he wore in each ear nearly blinded
me.

"Still trying to be like me, huh, Dorian? Since
when did you start wearing two earrings?"

"Man, please . . . I decided to go all out and
bling-bling tonight; it matches my wrist. What time
did you tell me to be ready?" he asked, showing me
his new Rolex.

I wasn't impressed; I expected him to wear one.

He lived in the most prestigious neighborhood
in the city and drove a 600 Mercedes. His business
was one of the biggest and most successful in the
state, but he never let it go to his head nor forgot
where he came from. We continued to maintain
our friendship even when he was playing professional football.

He had only been in the NFL two years when he got injured, and wasn't sure what to do next. He called Pop for advice and leadership.

Dorian was like another son to my parents. We'd shared dorm rooms throughout our four years at State University. In that short length of time, Dorian became my brother, and my family became the one he'd never had growing up.

When I was finishing up grad school, Dorian begged me to work for him. Actually he offered me more money than any other company. Almost twice as much. After much deliberation and prayer, I decided that I would make my own mark in the world and turned him down. He did, however, give me a new Benz and a graduation card with one thousand dollars in it as a gift. Now that's what friends are for.

"Hey, Koby!" Jackie called from the theatre room, "how's the new job going?"

"Hey, Jackie Chan! The new job is terrific."

Two small girls came running down the hall. "Uncle Koby! Uncle Koby!"

"Hey, Morgan! Hey, Meagan! Give Uncle Koby a kiss!" I scooped the girls into my arms. Morgan was five and looked just like her mother, and Meagan, who was three, mirrored her father.

"Where is Monica?" I asked, referring to their noticeably absent twelve-year-old sister.

"At a slumber party. You know she and Dorian are the only two around here with a Friday night social agenda." Jackie greeted me with a hug.

A full-figured, beautiful, brown-skinned woman with long hair, which she kept in a ponytail most of the time, Jackie was what most people call a good girl. Everyone loved her. Most people expected Dorian to marry some supermodel, diva type, but he married the very woman that captured his heart. Nevermind the fact that she already had two kids when he met her, he just took the ready-made family in stride, and he and Jackie continued making moves and growing together. They made a perfect pair.

"Still trying to hang at the club, huh, Koby? You still out there looking."

"No, Jackie. Ain't nobody *looking* for nothing. You know Dorian and I just go out there to chill and get our laugh on."

"Koby, don't mind her. And where did you meet the love of your life, dear wife of mine?—I believe we were at the club, if I recall."

"Number one, what makes you think you are the love of my life? And number two, if I recall we were *leaving* the club, not partying."

"Well, you were leaving because you already got your party on, right, Koby?"

"I refuse to get in the middle of this one," I said innocently.

"Punk, remind me to never use you as an alibi if I ever get into trouble," Dorian said. "And speaking of trouble, guess who I saw driving down the street today?"

"Ooh, I know, I know!" Jackie jumped up and down excitedly.

"Man, don't trip."

"Miss Rhea, Miss Rhea! That sho' is a pretty name," Dorian said mockingly.

Jackie pouted. "Aw . . . I wanted to guess."

"She called me earlier," I said.

"I just want both of you to remember my advising Koby a few months ago about that girl being no-good. But no, she was a bona fide diva, a fly-girl, a Miss Thang, café au lait, cream of the crop, wavy hair, small waist, curvy hips, perky breasts, pouty lips, every man's dream—straight-up ho!"

"Okay, Jackie. Dang!" I told her.

"Hold up, baby. Now you sound like a hater. And your wavy—what's up with that?"

"Shut up, Dorian, because this is one occasion where I can honestly say, 'I told you so.'"

Dorian shook his head. "Jackie, now that's just cold; you act like you're glad that they didn't work out."

"I am. She wasn't nothing but wannabe, high-class trash. I keep telling Koby, 'You gotta look on the inside as well as the outside; every woman that's fine ain't fair.'"

"True words if I ever heard them. Here! Here!" Dorian rallied, "And on that note, boo, Koby and I will be leaving. Baby girls, Daddy loves you. Give me a kiss." He bent down to kiss both girls.

"I'm gon' find an ugly, nice girl to please you, Jackie." I hugged her and smiled.

"She doesn't have to be ugly. Just make sure she isn't a gold-digging tramp." She stuck her tongue out at me. "You're better than that!"

"Jacqueline, my love, I am off to show the women what they missed out on because you snapped me up first." Dorian hugged his wife and whispered in her ear, "Now, be butt naked in the bed when I get back."

"Dorian, get out with your retarded self. Bye, Koby. Be safe," she said, kissing my cheek.

Dorian made sure the door was locked behind us. Then we jumped in his Benz and slid off.

Chapter 3

'Excuse Me, Miss' ("Take You Out")

—Luther Vandross

"Man, what is all of that?" Tim looked at the piping-hot plate as I removed it from the microwave.

"Leftovers from Momma's Sunday dinner: turkey, dressing, greens, yams, mac and cheese, cornbread, and, for dessert, homemade peach cobbler. Ha, ha! What you got?"

"Chicken pot pie, but it's a Stouffer's."

"Tim, grab a plate and get some of this food. You're not gonna make me feel bad by sitting there watching me eat all of this by myself."

Tim ran and got a paper plate and I shared my food with him. "Wow, this is good. Your Mom cooks like this every day?" he asked between bites.

"Heck no. Sunday is the only day of the week that she cooks. That is why she cooks such big meals—so my dad and brother can eat leftovers for the rest of the week. She has a pretty hectic schedule."

We were enjoying our home-cooked feast when Brenda popped her head in. "I hate to break up this wonderful display of male bonding, but I just received word that we have a meeting in an hour with Phil Barnes."

"Who's Phil Barnes?" I asked.

"He's a manager from the ninth floor," Tim told me.

"Ninth floor? That's engineering, right?"

"Yep." Brenda nodded.

"Why are we meeting with engineering?" I was still trying to figure out the method to the madness of my newfound employer. For the life of me, I couldn't figure out what engineering could possibly have to do with finance.

"Because Phil Barnes is a jerk who likes to throw his weight around," Tim said. "He claims it's because he feels that he needs to be made aware of what's going on with each department, but it's a total waste of time."

I figured as much but didn't say anything, especially since Brenda didn't seem pleased with Tim's response.

Brenda shook her head. "Just be in the video conference room on time. And, JaKoby, don't forget those reports."

"I got it covered," I assured her, and she walked out. "What was that all about?"

"Bureaucracy. These meetings stress her out, that's all. It's all crazy to me. Phil Barnes is an overrated windbag, who talks just to hear himself talk. Don't worry about it. Did you get your car back yet?"

"Naw, it'll be a coupla weeks or so."

"I wouldn't care, considering you're rolling in a Lexus as your loaner."

"Don't get me wrong, the Lex is a nice ride, but I miss my baby," I told him, cleaning off the table.

"Okay, tell me," he began, smiling, "whose fault was it?"

I stood up and began to walk out the break room. "This chick ran a light and hit my car."

He laughed. "Women drivers."

"Tell me about it. And get this—she didn't have any insurance." I sighed. Just that thought made me want to throw up.

"You're kidding. Man, I would be pissed."

"Believe me, I am, but what can I do? At least I had full coverage."

"Wait, what kind of car was it?"

I hesitated before answering, "A Benz."

I could still hear Tim laughing as I walked back to my office. I sat behind my desk and tried to focus on the forecasting reports that I was supposed to be working on, but I couldn't concentrate. I was grateful for the distraction when the phone on my desk began ringing. "JaKoby Jackson."

"Hey, Mr. Jackson," my insurance agent said.

"Gabe, how're things going?"

"Great. Look, the reason I was calling was because I have some news regarding your claim."

"Is there a problem?" I was hoping he wasn't going to tell me my car was beyond repair.

"No, no problem at all. I did find out that the woman that hit you indeed did have insurance."

"She did? Wow! That's good, I guess. Why did she tell me she didn't?" I wondered if Chryslin

Matthews was trying to run some type of game on him.

"Well, it turns out that her insurance didn't expire until midnight the day of the accident. She probably didn't even realize it at the time."

"That is good news."

"So, that's all I called to let you know. Everything's been taken care of as far as your car being repaired, and it should be ready in about three weeks or so."

"Thanks a lot, Gabe. I really appreciate it."

"No problem, JaKoby. You have a good day."

For some reason, the conversation with Gabe had my adrenaline pumping, and before I knew it, I had completed my reports in record time and was ready for the meeting with the dreaded Phil Barnes.

Tim had one thing right—Phil Barnes was definitely a talker—and most of what he said had nothing to do with the finance department. My mind kept drifting, and I almost fell asleep a couple of times. I didn't feel bad, when I looked over and saw that Tim was actually nodding off. Brenda noticed as well and didn't hesitate elbowing him awake. I didn't know who was more relieved when the meeting was adjourned, he or I.

"That wasn't that bad," I told Tim as we stood up to leave.

"Naw, that one was only an hour long. We've had some that lasted two and a half hours."

I couldn't imagine listening to Phil talk that long.

"Where did Brenda go?"

"She's probably somewhere running her mouth." Tim looked around the crowded conference room. "See . . . over there."

I looked over and was so shocked; I did a double-take. There was Brenda talking to none other than Chryslin Matthews. The two women were so caught up in their conversation that they didn't even look our way.

"Ain't this a blip," I said, not realizing I was talking out loud.

"What?"

"The woman that's talking to Brenda."

"Chrys." Tim shrugged.

"Chryslin Matthews, right?" I wanted to make sure we were talking about the same person.

"Yeah, she's an engineering assistant. A really nice girl, kinda quiet. How do you know her?"

"That's the chick that hit my car," I replied, still amazed that she was standing right across the room.

Neatly dressed in a white blouse and gray pin-striped skirt which stopped right above the knee, she was the picture of perfection. She was about 5-5 and what Dorian would call thick. She had meat in all the right places and seemed to glide in her black heels, which showed off her shapely legs. Her hair was pulled back with small curls framing her face. Her makeup was flawless, and she seemed very polished with her French manicured nails and silver jewelry. I loved women who achieved the elegant look, and Chrys looked like she managed that without even trying.

One of the things I liked about Rhea was that she kept a certain air of sophistication, but Rhea had nothing on the beautiful girl I was looking at now.

"The one without insurance?" Tim smiled. "Man, it's a small world. Well, at least you know she has a good job. Come on, let's go say hello."

We walked over to Brenda and Chryslin.

Tim interrupted their conversation. "Hi, Chrys. I think you already know JaKoby Jackson, the newest manager in finance?"

Chryslin looked as shocked to see me as I was to see her. Motionless, she stared at me as if she couldn't move.

"Nice seeing you again." I smiled.

"You two know each other?" Brenda asked.

Tim chuckled. "Yes, Chrys ran into JaKoby a little while back."

I looked over and gave him a threatening look. "Yes, we met before—how are you feeling?"

"I-I'm okay." She nodded. "How are you?"

"I'm good," I told her. "I'm glad to see you're okay."

"I didn't know you worked here," she said.

I could see her relaxing a bit more. "I've only been here a couple of weeks."

"That's good."

I wondered what she meant by that.

We continued to stare at each other for what seemed like hours. I had almost forgotten that Brenda and Tim were standing there. "Sorry to interrupt, but we need to get back downstairs," Brenda said.

"It was nice seeing you again, Ms. Matthews."

"Same here. And, please, call me Chrys."

"All right, Chrys." I couldn't stop smiling and prayed that I didn't look like a cornball.

"Bye, Chrys," Tim and Brenda said.

Chrys smiled back. "Enjoy the rest of your day."

There was no denying the attraction I was feeling. It was something I hadn't felt in a long time.

As soon as I got back to my desk, I clicked on the computer and typed the name in the employee database. Within moments, I found out Chryslin was an engineering assistant who reported to Phil Barnes. I was torn between e-mailing, calling, or instant messaging her. None of those options appealed to me as much as getting on the elevator and going to talk to her in person, so I set off to find her.

The first thing I noticed as I arrived on the engineering floor was how quiet it was. On our third-floor office, you could always hear people talking on the phone to customers or with each other, and people constantly walked around. I looked around and didn't see anyone. I tried to listen for voices, but the only thing I heard was the sound of what sounded like a copy machine.

There appeared to be two sides to the floor, one to the left of the elevator and one to the right. Both sides held what looked like rows of open cubes, but I didn't see any people anywhere. For a moment, it was eerie. I leaned and peaked down the empty hallway. Just as I turned to press the elevator button to leave, I heard a man laughing. Seconds later, I heard chatter. I continued toward the voices and came upon two women sitting at their desks.

"Excuse me, do you know where I could find Chryslin Matthews?"

"Sure," the first woman said. "She sits on the other side of the floor, third row in the middle."

"To the left of the elevators," the second woman offered.

I thanked them and headed in the direction that they sent me. Sure enough, there was Chryslin, leaning back in her chair, chatting on the phone. I stood back and leaned against the wall, waiting for her to finish her conversation.

"So now what am I supposed to do?" she said into the phone.

From the tone of her voice I could tell she was frustrated and wondered if this was the wrong time.

"But that's not helping me. I don't have time to deal with this now. I'll call you back."

She definitely ain't in the mood to chit chat, just send her an e-mail and call it a day. I decided to leave without being noticed.

"Hi."

I turned, and she was right behind me. "Hey, I'm sorry. I didn't mean to disturb you."

"You weren't disturbing me," she said. "What's going on?"

"Um, I got a call from my insurance agent."

"Oh goodness! Now what? Are you about to sue me . . . because it turns out that I did have insurance. I don't have any now, but I did at the time of the accident." She folded her arms.

"I know you did. No one is gonna sue you."

"Oh, okay."

"So what's going on with your car? Is it totaled?"

"Yeah. Now I have to go through the hassle of finding a new one. I have a rental until that happens."

"Well, my best friend owns a dealership—maybe he can help—Dorian Silver."

"The Dorian Silver. NFL Dorian Silver. Ha! You must think I make the big bucks like you. Name one car I can afford on his Mercedes Benz, BMW, Jaguar, Infiniti car lot?"

"Now, hold up. He has used cars too."

"I can't even afford a used anything on that lot."

"Whatever. If I'm not mistaken, that was a fairly new Camry you were driving."

"Okay, so I splurged a little on a *sedan*—that is a far cry from a Benz."

"Well, maybe I can use my pull and get you a deal."

"You must have a lot of pull to get my credit approved at Dorian Silver's!"

I gave her one of Dorian's cards and wrote the number to his personal line on the back. "Call him and let me know what kind of deal you get. You can thank me later."

Chapter 4

"Giving You the Best That I Got"

—Anita Baker

"Who is Chrys Matthews, and why is she calling me on my personal line?" Dorian asked as I sat in the afternoon traffic on the interstate, headed home.

"Just be nice," I told him.

"How nice?"

"Real nice."

"*Real* nice?"

"Look, *D*, she's a girl that works at the office with me."

"Well, well, well . . . no wonder you like your new job so much. Did you ask her out?"

"No, Dorian. We are just friends. I told you I gave her your card because I knew you'd look out. What did she say?"

"Whoa! A little anxious, huh, buddy?—'What did she say?'—What do you think she said?"

"Shut up, Dorian. You know what I mean. Did she mention me?"

"Yes, she said she works with you."

"Forget it."

"Fine then. I'll also forget what day she's coming by after work, so you won't *happen* to run into her."

"Come on, *D*, stop playing."

"Sounds like you're feeling her, Koby. What's up with her? Is she pretty? Yeah, she must be if you like her. You always go for them model-type chicks. I can picture her being light, bright, and damn-near white. Small, petite, and glamorous. Only wants salad and water when you go to dinner. As long as you are taking her to the mall and giving her money, she's happy."

"You know I'm not wasting my daytime minutes listening to this ignorance. I'm out!"

My cell rang back almost immediately. "Hang up on me again, Koby, and I'll call Rhea and tell her you want her to stop by tonight."

"Dorian, don't you have something better to do than to play on the phone?"

"A'ight, Koby. Dag! Can't even take a joke these days. When did you become so sensitive?"

"Some women find sensitivity attractive in a man—thank you."

"Yeah, the women that are attracted to weak men. See, a man like me, I'm hard."

"'Hard'? Okay, need I remind you of a certain man in a drunken stupor and crying on the floor because his girlfriend went away for the weekend and he didn't know where she was? Does the phrase, 'I love her and need to talk to her! Jackie, where are you?', ring a bell?" I asked, referring to the night that Jackie and her girlfriends decided to head to Atlantic City at the last minute. She'd left Dorian a note on his door: *Decided I needed some time to myself. Be back Monday.*

Dorian nearly died. He got so drunk that he passed out while giving this long speech about finally finding true love and happiness and how he had messed it up because he was afraid to commit. He just knew Jackie was out cheating on him. He probably felt guilty because although he loved Jackie, he was still out "doing his thing." I believe Jackie knew he was doing his thing too. I didn't know if she used this as a ploy to get *D* to straighten his ways, but after that weekend, Dorian made it clear to her and everyone else that he was going to marry her. (The two-carat ring he gave her was a key indicator.)

The next thing I knew, I was the best man in their wedding, and they had a baby on the way.

"That was the alcohol talking, stupid, not me, so before I waste any more of your precious daytime minutes, I'll be going now. Are you coming over to watch the game?"

"Yeah, because I know y'all have the good snacks. Oh, I forgot to tell you, I'll be needing your assistance this weekend. Jaamell and his friends want to go the Ja Rule concert at the Capital Centre. Momma suckered me into letting them stay at my house for the weekend. I also need to use the truck to pick them up too, I guess."

"You've lost your mind. You want me to spend my Saturday with not only knucklehead Jaamell, but his knucklehead friends too? To a concert three hours away? Now why would I want to do that?"

"It's called *giving back*, Dorian. Don't forget where you came from. Someone had to take time with you."

"Don't even try to give me that speech. Mama Jackson already gave it to me last week when she suckered me into helping. We already have the weekend planned. I figured we'd cookout at my crib on Friday night and watch a movie or two. Then, leave early Saturday morning for Capital City and hang out before the concert. I already talked Jackie into doing brunch on Sunday and then load 'em up and take 'em home."

"Boy, you are a genius. That's why you are my best friend . . . because you've always got a plan."

"Whatever. I'll see you tonight to watch your boys get whipped by the Packers."

"Wouldn't that be something—your boys winning a game. Stranger things have happened, I guess. I'll be there early for the snacks!"

"Peace."

The following Thursday, after work, I headed to meet Dorian at his car lot. I figured we could have a few drinks and hang out at happy hour for a while, since we wouldn't be able to go out on the weekend due to Jaamell and his buddies.

I swung into the lot and pulled alongside Dorian's Escalade. I spoke to Larry, the lot attendant, and entered the building. "Hey, Tracey," I said to the receptionist. "Dorian around?"

"Hey, JaKoby. Yeah, he's in the used lot with a customer."

"'Used lot'? Since when does Dorian sell cars?" I looked at her with surprise.

"Don't know, but he's selling 'em today."

I went through the side door to Dorian's used lot, which was more impressive than most new lots.

"Hey, Koby! What brings you out here?"

"I came to see if—" I stopped mid-sentence when I realized Chrys was standing next to him.

"Hey there," she called looking immaculate in jeans and a pink Polo top. She definitely filled the jeans perfectly, and her face was still the most beautiful I'd ever seen.

"Chrys . . . I'm surprised to see you here."

"Hey, you sent her to the best dealership in town, didn't you?"

"Yeah, I came to see how much pull you really have." Chrys winked at me.

"Well, what did you find?"

"Not much in my price range, that's for sure."

"Aw, come on now," Dorian told her. "We haven't even crunched the numbers yet."

"What do you like?" I asked her.

"I like a lot; that's not the problem."

"Tell you what . . . keep looking while Koby and I go inside to handle some business right quick."

"Okay, you and *Koby* take your time." She giggled.

"Look around," Dorian added, "and we'll be right back."

We went inside and he led the way to his office. The massive room was filled with trophies and plaques from his football career, awards from prestigious business organizations, and his well-earned degree from State University. His desk held several photos of Jackie and the girls.

"Koby, man, she is tight. I like her style. She is funny and smart, and she can hold up her end of a conversation. I definitely wouldn't have pictured you liking her. This one may be a keeper though. Koby with a thick girl—who would have thought it? Wait till I call Pop! You just ran into her at work?"

"It's more like she ran into me before I even got the job."

"Huh?"

"She's the woman that ran into my car."

"The one with no insurance?"

"Yeah, and she did have insurance, come to find out."

"Wait a sec—she's the woman that hit your car, and you're here helping her get a new one?"

"Yeah, that's about it." I shrugged.

"Yeah, you're definitely feeling this chick, Koby, because that's crazy as hell. Well, are you gonna ask her out? At least, get her number. It's about time you get with someone you can really enjoy, and who knows, she may just be the one. She's not a chickenhead; at least we know that."

"Let me do this, okay? I know what I'm doing. There are a lot of things to consider. First of all, there are work ethics involved."

"But you work on different floors in different departments."

"I know what I'm doing, man. Besides, I don't even know if she's got a man already."

"A'ight, it's your thing. Now let's go help your *colleague* find a car."

We went back outside where Chrys was laughing with Larry. "Find anything?" I asked.

"Well, I'm really feeling the black J30, but my pockets are really feeling the Acura; I think I'll test-drive that."

"Sure thing. Larry, can you go grab the keys for her?" Dorian asked.

"Be right out with them." Larry went to get the keys.

"Well, I am gonna get out of here and let you guys take care of business."

Chrys looked at me. "Okay, I guess I'll see you at the office tomorrow."

Dorian added, "In your new ride, of course."

She turned to Dorian. "Ha! You haven't seen my credit application yet. Don't forget you promised not to laugh."

"Madame, whose name is on the big marquee out front?"

"I believe it's yours, Mr. Silver," Chrys answered.

"Then we'll make it happen."

"Good luck, Chrys. Dorian, I'll holla at you later."

I decided I would go to the grocery store to stock up for my weekend houseguests. Just then my cell phone rang. "Hello."

"Hey, bro. I know you're getting hyped about chilling with us this weekend."

"Hey, Jaamell. What's up?"

"Nothing much. Ma told me to call and confirm what time you'll be here tomorrow."

"Probably around four. Hopefully I'll be able to leave work early."

"Wow! You? Leaving work early? I don't believe it. You must really be excited about the weekend."

"Don't flatter yourself, *J.* I'm just not trying to get caught up in the traffic. By the way, who do you have coming to my house?"

"My boys, Koby?"

"What boys? I know Mark is coming. You wouldn't dare go anywhere without him," I said, referring to his best friend.

"Shut up, Koby. You and Dorian act like y'all are joined at the hip too. But, yeah, Mookie, my boy Chief, and my boy G-Wash."

"Wow! *J,* Mookie, Chief, and G-Wash—I can hardly wait," I said, unexcited.

"So tomorrow at four."

"Be ready, *J,* 'cuz I will leave y'all." I wanted him to know I wasn't playing.

"A'ight, Koby. Tell Dorian be ready to get whupped up on the Xbox."

"Yeah, yeah, yeah. Tell him yourself."

"Bye, Koby."

"See ya, *J.*"

After grocery shopping and picking up some Chinese take-out, I headed home. Before I could make it, my cell rang again. "Hello."

"Koby, it's Dorian. Chrys is still here finishing up some paperwork, and I need you to do me a quick favor."

"What's up?"

"Well, you know she has a rental car. Well, I told her there was no need to keep it another day now that she has her new ride. Since you live right by the airport, can you meet her at the rental place when she turns in the car and give her a ride back here?"

"What are you up to, *D*? I don't need you to play matchmaker. I told you I got this." I couldn't believe Dorian was setting me up, but I was still glad.

Chrys yelled in the background, "I told him I can wait until tomorrow to turn it in. It's no big deal."

"No problem. Tell her I can be there in fifteen minutes. Which rental company did she use?"

Dorian gave me the name, and I headed toward the airport. I hit the disc changer, and the sound of Maxwell's "Get to Know Ya" flowed through the speakers. *Isn't that ironic*, I thought, as I pulled into the return section of the rental area and tried to relax. *Just be cool, Koby. Be yourself. Don't try too hard. Just let everything flow.* I decided to say a quick prayer to calm my nerves.

I opened my eyes just in time to see Chrys headed toward me. I must've looked crazy because when she opened the door to the truck and got in, she asked, "Were you sleeping? I told Dorian I could wait and not to bother you, but he insisted that you wouldn't mind."

"No, I was just—never mind. Did you get everything taken care of?"

"Yep. I just have to go back to the dealership and pick up my new ride."

"And what type of ride would that be?"

"My candy apple red Acura."

"Oh, I thought you wanted the Infiniti?" I asked, wondering why Dorian didn't sell her the J30 she mentioned.

"I told you I couldn't afford that car. It's amazing that I got the Acura. Somehow your boy worked his magic, and my payments are even lower than the payments on the Camry I had. I'm gonna miss that car though. That was my first *new* car."

I tried to concentrate on driving, although I wanted to look at her. "Hey, now you got a great car. I mean, it may be used, but it's better."

"Yep, he's in the blessing business."

"I hope you mean God and not Dorian."

"Of course, silly. But, He did use Dorian to bless me. Well, actually He used *you* to use Dorian to bless me."

"A'ight, now you are getting a bit confusing."

"Hey, I am a firm believer in six degrees of separation. And now that I know you and you know Dorian Silver, there really isn't anyone in this world that I can't meet. How do you know him?"

I proceeded to tell her the history of our friendship. We laughed so hard and seemed to enjoy the ride so much that we were both surprised when I got to the dealership.

"You guys are so crazy."

I pulled into the parking lot and looked for the car. "Where is your new ride?"

"Dorian said he was going to have Larry shine it up and remove the stickers, but I don't see it."

We walked around back, where we saw the Acura parked with the stickers still on it. We returned to the front of the building and searched for Larry, who happened to be coming from out of the garage.

"Hey, Larry," I called to him, "why didn't you do Chrys' car yet?"

"I did do it, Koby; it's sitting right out front."

"No, it's not." Chrys tried not to seem worried. "It's still sitting there with the sale sticker on it."

"I know I cleaned that car. I am not crazy."

"And we aren't either, Larry," I told him. "Where is Dorian?"

"He left after he finished her paperwork. He left a note for you though, Koby. Come on, Chrys, 'cuz I know this car is sitting right out front." They left out to find the invisible car.

At the moment I opened the note from Dorian, I heard Chrys scream. I ran out to see what happened. I found her standing next to her new black Infiniti J30, while Larry was looking at her like she was crazy. I looked down at the note:

I made it happen, now it's your turn.
For once look on the inside and you might find happiness.
Your Brother,
D
p.s. Make sure your girl gets some insurance!

I smiled and looked at Chrys, who by this time was crying as she looked at her paperwork. She ran and hugged me, saying, "You really have got some pull!"

Chapter 5

"Un-Break My Heart"

—Toni Braxton

I had to admit, I really enjoyed my weekend with Jaamell and his friends. The concert was off the hook, and of course, the boys were excited to be hanging with Dorian Silver. We enjoyed watching movies and playing video games at his house. We even had a heart-to-heart with the boys, to stress the important issues like staying in school and making the grades, and staying out of trouble too.

Dorian let them know that his NFL career was a one-in-a-million opportunity, but it was getting his degree and being a good husband and father that made him successful. He told them those were the qualities that Pop taught him. It made me proud to hear him speaking of my father that way.

We even openly talked about sex, drugs, and alcohol. I told the guys about the proper way to treat a lady and encouraged them to abstain from having sex or to, at least, have enough respect for the woman to wait until she was ready. I really believe we had an impact on the little posse.

Jackie went out of her way, fixing a dynamic seafood brunch for us on Sunday. But as much as I enjoyed bonding with the boys, I was glad to have the house back to myself on Sunday evening.

A knock at the door was the last thing I was expecting. "Hey, Koby."

"Hey, Rhea. What brings you over here?"

"I wanted to see you. I mean, I really want us to sit down and talk."

"Rhea, I am really tired. Jaamell and his friends have been here all weekend. I'm just getting back from taking them home. This might not be the best time to talk."

"Oh, how is Jaamell?"

"He's fine. *D* and I took them to the concert at the Capital Centre."

"I bet that was fun. I wish I could've gone." Rhea put her hands in her back pockets.

I forced myself not to look because I knew what she was trying to do—draw attention to her perfect derriere. "Yeah, it was pretty cool."

She tilted her head. "How are your parents?"

"Fine."

"I can see you're not much for conversation, so I guess I'll go."

"Okay, Rhea, I'm sorry. I'm just tired and—"

The next thing I knew, Rhea's mouth was on mine, her tongue searching for my open mouth. Her hands were around my waist and pulling me closer to her. Somehow my hands were stroking her hips. She caressed the center of my back as she pulled my shirt up, and I fingered her full breasts, arousing her nipples with my thumbs. She began to rub her thigh between my legs, and I felt myself getting harder with each passing moment.

Finding the front of my jeans, she quickly undid my belt and felt around until she found what she was looking for, stroking me with an expert's touch.

I quickly lifted her blouse and began sucking her breast through her lace bra. I had no doubt that she had on a matching thong. She knew I got off on that, and the thought of it made me want her more. I lifted the bra and gently bit on her breasts, taking each nipple hungrily into my mouth.

Rhea had my pants down to my knees, and by now we were ready to take it a step further.

"Koby, damn! I missed you, baby," she whispered in my ear. She gently licked my earlobe and along my neck.

"Damn, Rhea," was all I could say. But then a flash of her kissing another man as they waited outside of a restaurant entered my mind. She had licked *his* earlobe too. The ache I felt in my chest quickly snapped me back into reality. I grabbed her wrists. "Hold up, Rhea. Stop! I can't do this."

"Yes, you can, baby. See"—She wrapped her fingers around my swollen head—"you want to."

"No, I don't. Really, I don't. Maybe you should just leave."

"Koby, we've gotta talk about this . . . please, baby. I've apologized a hundred times. I love you so much." Tears poured out of her eyes and ran down her cheeks.

"Rhea, you cheated. You jeopardized what we had for another man. I told you, 'I am not competing for anyone.' I did everything I was supposed to do in the relationship. Everything. I gave my all. I went above and beyond, and it still wasn't enough for you . . . obviously. You wanted more, remember? I don't have any more to give." I pulled up my pants and straightened my clothes.

"Koby," she cried, "I really wasn't thinking straight, baby. Please, try to understand. Don't do this. We can work it out, I promise. It will never happen again. Koby, you know we are a great team. What about all of our plans?"

"Correction, Rhea—we *were* a great team, and you canceled those plans when you decided to sleep with your boss. Now, please leave!"

She got herself together and moped out of my house, leaving me sitting on the side of the couch, staring.

Chapter 6
"Ordinary People"
—John Legend

Thursday afternoon found me with no one to eat with and no lunch to eat. My usual lunch mate, Tim, was on vacation, and Brenda had a conference call.

I decided to run out to the deli around the corner and grab a sandwich. The waitress had just given me my tray, and as I turned to find an empty seat, I noticed Chrys sitting alone at a table by the window. "Hey, you," I greeted her as I walked to her table.

"Hey, yourself. I haven't seen you around. How've you been?"

"Great. We have been slammed with meetings and conference calls this week."

"Sit down." She motioned to the empty chair.

I sat across from her and began to pick nervously at my food.

Chrys, on the other hand, heartily ate her sandwich and chips. She looked at me picking at my sandwich. "What's wrong? Your food's not good?"

"No, it's okay." I smiled and took a bite. "How are you enjoying your new ride?"

"Now you know it's the bomb. I can't thank you enough. People keep asking me how I got it."

"And what are you telling them?"

"I've been saying exactly what it is—a ridiculous blessing."

"You go, girl!" I laughed. "Did you put it on the road this weekend?"

"As a matter of fact, I rode to Capital City this past weekend."

"Wow! It's a small world because I was in Capital City myself this weekend."

"Really?"

"Yeah, Dorian and I took my little brother to a concert."

She smiled. "That's so sweet."

After we talked a little while longer, she stood. "Gotta go. As usual, I have enjoyed myself. And, again, thanks for using your pull; hopefully, one day I can return the favor."

"Okay, how about dinner tomorrow and we'll call it even?"

She looked surprised and took a moment to think about it. "Sure, I'd like that."

"Great. I'll call you tonight and set it up. Can I get your number?"

"How about I get yours and give you a call?" She bit her bottom lip, looking seductive without even trying.

I pulled out one of my business cards and wrote my home and cell numbers on the back.

She read the card and smiled. "Wow! You really want me to call, huh?"

"If you don't, you'll find yourself driving a Hyundai."

"Imagine that! I'll call you later." She grinned at me, grabbed her purse, and waved as she got into her car, which I didn't even notice when I first got to the deli.

The rest of the day flew by.

Before I knew it, my phone was ringing as I was getting out of the shower around 9 o'clock. I looked on the caller ID. I took a deep breath and answered, trying to sound calm, cool, and collected, as Pops would say. "Hello."

"Hello. May I speak to JaKoby Jackson, please?"

"Who's calling?"

"Chrys Matthews."

"Let me see if he's available." I paused and tried not to laugh. "He said call him back later."

"Oh, not a problem."

"I'm just kidding. It's me."

"You'd better be glad you said something . . . because I wasn't calling you back."

"Why not?"

"Oh, you want me to sweat you?—I don't think so." She laughed.

"So, basically, I'm not worth sweating?"

"Uh . . . no!"

We talked past one in the morning. She told me about growing up as an only child in Georgia. I told her about my family and also about being an only child for most of my childhood. We talked about books, movies, music, and anything else that came to mind. Soon, it felt like we were old friends.

She yawned. "Okay, I have got to get off this phone or I am going to oversleep."

"I hear that. I can't believe we talked this long, though I really enjoyed it. So . . . what time do you want me to pick you up tomorrow night?"

"How about we meet somewhere?"

"Sure. Where do you want to meet?" I wanted to ask why but didn't, thinking that maybe she didn't feel comfortable enough with me to let me know where she lived.

"How about Putt-Putt, by the mall?"

"Miniature golf?" I wanted to make sure I heard her correctly.

"Yeah, miniature golf. What did you have in mind?"

"No, that's cool. What time?"

"Seven-thirty okay?"

"Seven-thirty it is. I'll see you tomorrow. Sweet dreams."

"You too."

I hung up the phone and fell asleep with visions of Chrys and miniature golf in my head.

The next day, I woke up with a smile on my face, knowing I would be spending time with her that night. Friday was usually the most exhausting day for me at work, but I was far from exhausted when five o'clock rolled around. I wanted to go by Chrys' desk and see her but didn't want to seem anxious. I hung around briefly after work and then decided to go by and talk to Dorian for a minute to kill time.

"Koby, my man, what brings you by here? You trying to hang out tonight?"

"Nope. Got a date."

"A date?" He looked surprised.

"Is there an echo in here? You heard me—a date." I tried not to smile.

"Well, Rhea finally got to you, huh? What did she do—come over and throw it on you real good?"

"It's not with Rhea."

"Not with Rhea?"

"It's with Chrys."

"With Chrys?"

"Yeah, I'm taking her to Putt-Putt."

"Putt-Putt?"

"You really gotta do something about that echo. Yes, she wants to play miniature golf."

"Well, at least she's a cheap date."

"Bye, Dorian. I'm out."

"Let me know how it goes."

I had just gotten home and was about to jump in the shower, when the phone rang. I checked the caller ID and saw Rhea's number. I tossed the cordless phone on the bed and let it ring.

As I was getting dressed, I got an idea. I grabbed the box out of the back closet and tossed a blanket inside. I reached in the kitchen cabinet and got two wine glasses and two small plates. I stopped by the grocery store and placed some fresh cut melon, grapes, and strawberries in the shopping cart. Then I got some cheese, cold cuts, a loaf of French bread, and a chilled bottle of Merlot. I quickly remembered napkins, grabbed a knife from the kitchen aisle, and finished my list with a package of gourmet chocolate.

"Wow! Someone is in for a treat tonight." The cashier winked at me as she bagged my items.

"I hope so." I smiled back at her.

"For your girlfriend?"

"No, a friend."

"Well, after all of this, she'll be your girlfriend."

I paid for my groceries and arranged everything in the box under the blanket. I placed the box in my trunk, and noticing it was five minutes after seven, sped to meet my date. I arrived exactly at 7:27 and parked next to her shiny black car. "Hey, you're early," I said out of my passenger window.

"To be early is to be on time, to be on time is to be late, and to be late is to be left out, my dear."

"I heard that."

We got out of our vehicles and walked inside to get our golfing gear for the evening. After getting our clubs, score cards, and balls, we headed out to start the game.

The fall air was perfect, not too cold with just a hint of a breeze. Chrys looked fabulous as usual in a blue wind suit, Nike T-shirt, and matching Air Max. Her hair was pulled high on top of her head, with curls coming down, and her face was flawless with just the right amount of makeup.

"Do you play golf?" she asked as I prepared to putt.

"No, my dad and his brother do. They've been asking me to come out so I can learn." I swung at the ball and completely missed it.

She giggled. "You might want to take them up on their offer. Tell you what—how about we play for fun, and don't worry about the score?"

I missed again. "Okay, I think that's a good idea."

She lined herself up professionally to take a shot, carefully eyeing her target. She gracefully swung the club and missed the ball!

I threw my head back and laughed. "Ha, ha, ha, ha!"

She turned and looked at me with a disgusted grin. She swung again and made a hole in one. "He who laughs last laughs best." She placed her hands on her hips and stuck her tongue out at me. Little did she know how sexy she looked.

"Okay, did you eat Chinese food today or something?" I asked her.

"No. Why?"

"Because that is the second fortune cookie you quoted tonight."

"Oh, you still got jokes, huh? We'll see who you quote after I whip you in this game."

"Hey, you said we were playing for fun."

"Winning will be fun for me!" She grinned.

We played three rounds, and by the time I got the hang of it, it was time for the course to close. I couldn't believe how quickly the time went by.

As we walked out to our cars, I asked her, "Are you hungry?"

"Sure. I could go for something, but isn't it kind of late?"

"Leave that up to me. Well . . . you wanna drive, or you want me to?"

"You mean leave my new ride out here? Have you lost your mind?"

"You can park it over in the grocery store parking lot. I'll follow you over there, and then I'll drive."

After she parked her car, I opened the door so she could get into my car.

She smiled. "Who said chivalry is dead?"

"What do you want to listen to?"

"Where are we going?"

"Chill and enjoy the ride. Now what are you in the mood to hear?"

"Do you have Mary *J*?"

"Uh . . . I don't smoke," I said, switching the disc changer.

"*Funny*—I mean Mary J. Blige, Mr. Comedian."

"Right here."

"Hit track seven, please."

Soon we were singing along with Mary, and by the end of the song, we were both holding our sides from laughing so hard.

"Where are you taking me?"

"We're almost there. Didn't I tell you to calm down?" I turned onto a secluded road, passing the "Private Property" signs along the way, and followed it all the way back to a small lake sitting behind a well-lit house. "Hold tight." I told her as I popped open the trunk and got out. I grabbed the box and walked near the lake, where I spread the blanket and arranged everything neatly on top. I walked back to her side, opened the door, and grabbed her hand to help her out of the car.

She whispered, "Isn't this trespassing?" and grabbed a hold of my arm.

I whispered back, "Not if you have the owner's consent," and put my arm around her waist.

She continued to whisper. "You know the owner?"

I continued to whisper too. "Yes. See the back of that big house?"

"Yeah."

"That's Dorian peeping out of the back window at us."

"Get out of here! Stop playing!" She whispered a little louder. "Then why are you whispering?"

I whispered back, "Because you are."

My cell phone rang as I was leading her to the romantic feast I had prepared or, shall I say, bought. I hit the talk button on my phone. "What, man?"

Dorian laughed in my ear. "You all right back there?"

"Why are you calling?"

"I just wanted to say hi to Chrys and check on her car."

"I am hanging up now!"

"Handle your business."

I hung the phone up.

Chrys turned to look at me and the picnic. "Koby, this is so special."

"Have a seat."

She sat on the blanket and leaned back on her hands. "I can't believe this! No one has ever done this for me before."

"That's because no one else is me. Oh shoot, hold up—" I ran back to open the trunk and took out the portable CD boom box. I grabbed the jazz mix CD I had been saving for an occasion such as this and returned to the blanket.

Chrys was giggling to herself.

"What's funny?"

"Dorian is standing on the deck waving at us."

I turned around just in time to see him duck and scurry in the back door. "I am going to kill him." I let the CD play.

"That's kinda violent, JaKoby; you should consider anger management." She tucked a strawberry into her mouth. A little juice ran out of the corner of her mouth, and I grabbed a napkin and wiped it.

"Ooh, sorry, but this is so good." She licked her lips.

We feasted on sandwiches and fruit, drank wine, listened to fine music, and talked under the stars until she looked at her watch and said, "Wow! It's 3 a.m. I need to go."

"Why? Come on, I am having the greatest time with you." I rubbed her arm.

"I am too. This has definitely been one of the most perfect evenings I've ever had in my life. It will probably be *the* most perfect evening in my life." She got up and stretched.

I reached to her and pulled her close to me. She smelled as sweet as I imagined, and I buried my face in her neck.

She gently hugged me back. "We'd better get this cleaned up so we can get out of here."

"Can't we go somewhere else and talk?"

"Koby, we just talked for seven and a half hours. Aren't you talked out?" she asked as we both folded the blanket.

I pulled my end, which caused her to fall towards me, and looked into her eyes. "I could talk to you forever, Chryslin Matthews."

She quickly looked away. "Come on, we gotta get out of here." She grabbed my hand, and we walked back to the car.

I put the box and the radio in the trunk, and we drove back to the parking lot in silence.

"Chrys," I said as I walked her to the car, "I have

had the most perfect night of my life, and I want to see you again . . . if that's okay with you."

"Hey, no need for formalities, Koby. We are friends, right? I'll call you tomorrow." She hugged me tight for what seemed like a long while, kissed my cheek, and got into her car. She waved out the window and left me standing in the parking lot.

Chapter 7

"Vision of Love"

—Mariah Carey

Over the next few weeks, Chrys became an integral part of my life. We generally kept it "strictly business" at work. Neither one of us wanted to put our business out there, but we would occasionally "happen to meet" at the deli for lunch. We had our nightly phone talks, which lasted way past one, sometimes two in the morning. We would even do the "you've-got-mail" thing and chat online at work and at home.

Ironically enough, as much as we saw each other and talked, we never went on a formal date. We would just decide to meet at the movies or bowling alley. She even had us meeting at the arcade to play video games. I never asked why I couldn't pick her up, but it bothered me that she never wanted me to.

When I brought up my concerns about Chrys to Dorian, he told me, "Maybe she just wants to take things slow."

"But she's never invited me over, *D*. You don't think something's up with that?"

"Maybe she's a virgin—have you thought about that?"

"What? She's not a virgin . . . well . . . I don't think she is," I said, wondering if that could be the case.

"Look, why don't you just suggest coming over one night? Ask her to cook."

I sighed. "Yeah, maybe."

"If it bothers you, then talk about it; don't be acting paranoid."

I decided to take his advice.

"Hey, why don't we hang out at your place tonight?" I asked her one Saturday afternoon as we were walking through the park eating ice cream cones.

"My place?" She looked at me quizzically.

"Sure. We can rent movies, eat pizza, and cuddle on the sofa. Do you have a sofa?"

She smirked. "Yes, I have a sofa. And I have a chaise lounge too."

"Big willie—a chaise lounge." I rubbed the back of her neck with my thumb.

Things hadn't really gotten physical between us. We would hold hands and hug; outside of brief kisses on the cheek or quick goodbye pecks, that was as far as it got. Ironically, I still had an intense passion for her.

I understood taking things slow, but I at least deserved the opportunity to taste her mouth. No doubt, I was attracted to her physically, and restraining myself was a task. My phone rang as I was thinking. "Hello," I answered, without first looking at who was calling.

"Hey, Koby. Are you busy?" Rhea asked.

"Yeah, actually I am."

"I really need to talk to you, Koby; it's important. Can I meet you somewhere?" she whined.

"I don't think that's a good idea." I tried to play it off because Chrys was standing right next to me.

"Koby, are you with a girl?—you sound funny."

"That's none of your business," I growled. "I gotta go."

"Koby, please—"

I hit *end* as she was yelling. I turned to Chrys, who had a sly grin on her face.

"Woman problems?"

"More like nerve problems."

"Well, well, well . . . that's the territory that comes with being a 'mack.' And I thought you were one of the good guys." She laughed. "What did you do to her to cause her to get on your nerves?"

"I believe it's called *treating her right*, but she didn't want me when I was doing that."

"Oh, and now she is trying to get you back, huh?"

"Of course. You know how women are—never miss the water until the well runs dry. And, besides, you got me now."

"Please . . . I guess I'm supposed to be thrilled because her loss is my gain, right?"

"And you know this."

My phone rang again. This time I made sure to check before answering. "What's up, *D*?"

"Where you at, Koby?"

"City Park with Chrys."

"Do you ever take her anywhere nice?" He laughed.

"Look, I take her wherever she wants to go," I replied, admiring her as she licked her cone.

"Let me holler at her for a minute."

I passed the phone to Chrys and tried to eavesdrop.

"Hey . . . Yeah . . . I know . . . Thanks . . . Sure . . . Sounds like fun . . . Uh-huh . . . Don't say that . . . Okay, if he wants to . . . I'll see you then. Here's Koby. Bye." She laughed as she passed the phone to me.

"What's so funny?" I asked suspiciously.

"Just talk to Dorian."

"*D*, what's so funny?"

"I don't know what you're talking about; I just invited you guys over for dinner and a movie tonight. You game?"

"Sure. I had just suggested dinner and a movie. What time?"

"You tell me."

I looked over at Chrys and asked her what a good time was for her.

I told Dorian, "We'll be there around six."

"Cool. I'll let Jackie know," he said and hung up.

"Now, what was so funny?" I grabbed her arm jokingly.

She took her ice-cream and pushed it into my nose. "*That* is funny!" she said and ran as I chased after her.

Chrys insisted on picking me up that evening. "Come on, you've never ridden in my new car, and besides, it'll give you the chance to be chauffeured for a change. I know, in all of your 'treating women right,' you always drive."

"I told you I can come and get you."

"Nope. Just give me directions and be ready when I get there at 5:30."

"Is there some reason why you don't want me to see your house?"

"Don't be silly, Koby. I just offered to drive."

"Fine. How about I drive to your place and then you can drive your car when I get there?"

"That's crazy, and a waste of gas."

"Well, I'm crazy about you, and it's my gas."

Chryslin inhaled deeply. "Fine. Meet at my house at 5:30."

As I turned on her street, I scolded myself for being mistrustful of her. *Now that she's comfortable enough with me coming to her house, she may be comfortable enough to do other things.*

When I pulled up to her address, she was already waiting beside her car, looking attractive and holding a yellow rose. "Your chariot awaits, sir." She smiled. "And for you, a yellow rose . . . for friendship."

"My, my, my . . . I'm impressed. No date has ever given me roses before." I grinned.

"I aim to please. Are you ready? You're a little early."

"To be early is to be on time."

"Hey, you haven't been eating Chinese today, have you?"

"No, aren't you going to invite me in for a drink or something?"

"No, thanks. I'm good."

"I wanted to see your place."

"I'm not ready for you to see it yet; besides, I can show you later."

I raised my eyebrows. "'Later'?"

"Yeah. I know, in your effort to treat me right, you will be offering to come over to cook dinner, right?"

"Darn! I thought it was gonna be a surprise."

I locked my doors, and we got into her car.

"What do you wanna hear?" she asked.

"Got any Mary *J*?"

"I don't smoke," she said and put in the CD. We did our regular sing-along routine.

I could barely give her directions to Dorian's because I was laughing so hard. "Wait! Back up, back up! You passed the house!"

"Which one?"

"Hit reverse. The brick one with the fountain."

She backed up in the middle of the street and pulled into Dorian's circular driveway. He and Jackie were standing outside as we parked. They watched in amusement as Chrys got out, walked to my side of the car, and opened the door for me.

"Hey, how did y'all pass the house?" Dorian asked.

Chrys and I looked at each other and cracked up.

"Ms. Speed Demon here," I said when I finally caught my breath.

Chrys laughed. "But weren't you the one giving directions?"

"Hi, Chrys. I'm Jackie, Dorian's wife. I've heard so much about you."

"Hi. It's a pleasure to meet you."

Chrys was noticeably impressed when we went in. "Your house is so beautiful. Oh, your kids are beautiful too." She admired the photos of the girls, which were hanging throughout the foyer. "Are they here?"

"No. We wanted you to come over and enjoy your first visit. We didn't want you going home and telling your friends, 'Dorian Silver got some bad-ass kids! I went to his house and couldn't even eat in peace.'" Dorian led us into the den, where Chrys and I sat on the leather sectional.

"I would never say that," Chrys said. "I used to work at a daycare center. I love kids."

"But you don't work there now, do you? You learned real fast that kids are bad." Jackie laughed.

"Stop! Seriously, I love kids."

"And where are yours?" I asked Chrys.

"Believe me, I'm going to have one some day."

"'One'?"

Dorian and Jackie looked at each other and chuckled.

"Kids are like potato chips"—I looked at her—"You can't have just one; that's no fun."

She put her hands on her hip and directed her eyes toward me. "And just where is your clan, Mr. Jackson?"

"Believe me, when I meet the love of my life, we will have a clan, Ms. Matthews." I looked deep into her eyes to let her know I meant it.

Dorian sighed. "To be young and in love . . ."

"Shut up, *D.*" I never broke my stare, but Chrys looked away quickly.

"Well, I have to go finish dinner. Dorian, quit being rude and offer our guest something to drink."

"What would you like to drink, Chrys?" Dorian asked.

I stood up. "Hey, what about me?"

"Oh, my bad—Koby can you get Chrys and me a drink?"

"Ever the comedian, huh, D?"

"Do you need help with anything, Jackie?" Chrys offered.

"Not really, but I could use some company in the kitchen. Come on, girl."

They went into the kitchen, leaving Dorian and me to ourselves.

"I like her," Dorian said; "she's good for you."

"Gee, thanks for your approval. But, seriously, I like her too."

"I can tell."

"I really want this to work."

"Then make it work. Keep doing what you're doing and be yourself—it's working now."

"How can you tell?"

"Because, you've been seeing the girl for weeks and barely spent twenty dollars on her, and she's still with you. Plus, Jackie likes her! Remember, a woman's intuition."

Dorian was right—Jackie loved Chrys. We heard them laughing and talking from the kitchen. At one point we went inside to see what they were doing, and they instantly kicked us out.

After an amusing dinner, we settled into the

theatre room. "What do you want to watch?" Dorian asked.

"What do you like, Chrys?" Jackie asked. "And don't say, 'Whatever,' because *Dumb* and *Dumber* will pick something stupid like *The Mack* or *Superfly*."

"What are you talking about, girl? Those are classics," Dorian told her.

"I wasn't gonna say either one of those," I said; "I was gonna suggest *Shaft*."

"Shut your mouth!" Dorian hooted.

"See, Chrys—it's a competition of who can be the goofiest." Jackie shook her head at us.

"Oh, I get it now, Jackie. Well, Koby has got my vote!"

"No, I think Dorian has got him beat!"

"Forget both of you," Dorian said. "I don't hear either one of you making a suggestion."

"Chrys?" I looked over at her.

"I get to pick anything?" she asked.

"We're not watching *Steel Magnolias* or *Pretty Woman* or anything like that," I warned.

"Or *The Color Purple*!" Dorian added.

"Ooh, yeah! Pick one of those, girl!" Jackie clapped her hands.

"Naw, I've got a good one." Chrys had a knowing look on her face.

"What is it?" I asked.

"Come here, Jackie." Chrys whispered into her ear.

Jackie threw her head back with laughter. "Now *that* is a classic. Be right back, fellas."

"You better not have picked anything crazy like *I'm Gonna Git You Sucka* either," Dorian said.

We all got comfortable as Jackie set the movie

up. She dimmed the lights and rushed in and sat next to her husband. Dorian and I roared with laughter when the opening scenes of *Purple Rain* came on the screen.

The evening came to a perfect end as I stepped out of Chrys' car. I walked around and opened the door for her to get out.

She smiled. "You're such a gentleman."

"Well, I certainly have enjoyed you. Two great dates in one day; that is really outstanding." I wrapped my arms around her.

She looked up at me. "Yeah. I rarely have two great dates in one *month*."

I leaned my forehead against hers and closed my eyes. She leaned toward me and kissed me softly on the lips. It felt so perfect. I opened my mouth and nibbled on her lips.

She gently pulled away. "So . . . I'll talk to you tomorrow?"

"You sure you don't want me to come in?"

"No, it's late." She looked at me with desire in her eyes.

"I really want you to come in; I promise I won't bite." I touched her face.

"I know you don't."

"No, I do, but tonight I won't . . . unless you want me to."

"Why, JaKoby Jackson, I do believe you're getting fresh with me." Chrys spoke in her best Southern drawl. "No. I'm gonna go."

"Well, at least let me walk you to your door." I held her hand as we walked.

"Thank you, but I'm fine." She hugged me and kissed me softly again. "Call me when you get home."

I watched her run up the small walkway and unlock her door, leaving me standing in the driveway.

Chapter 8

"Certainly"

—Erykah Badu

Thanksgiving was fast approaching, and I had a lot to be thankful for. The Lord had blessed me with so much—I had my health, my family, a great job, and a beautiful woman. My life had taken such a turn for the better since last year. My parents were hosting Thanksgiving dinner at their house and Dorian and Jackie were going to host Christmas. This year, I had planned to share both holidays with Chrys by my side.

"Dorian told us that your new friend is nice," Pop told me one night on the phone.

"She is, Pop; I'm real excited about you all meeting her."

"Well, that's good, son. It's nice when you are excited about a woman. So tell me, is she a whipper snapper too?"

"Naw, Pop. Just the opposite; she's like no other woman I've met in my life, and she makes me smile."

"Wow! She must be something. I can't wait to meet her."

"Me either, Pop. I'll see you on Thursday, okay?"

The night before Thanksgiving, I called Chrys. "Hey, what are you doing?" I could hear a lot of noise in the background.

"Hey, I gotta call you back," she said, sounding flustered.

"What's wrong?"

"Nothing. I'm just in the middle of something right now."

"You sure you're okay?" I asked, sensing something wasn't right.

"Yeah, I'll call you back soon."

Later on, I tried to reach her again but didn't get an answer at her house or on her cell phone. When I hadn't heard from her by eleven that night, I became worried. I tried to reach her again, to no avail.

Dorian called to see what time we were leaving for Momma's. I told him I couldn't find Chrys and about what happened when I talked to her hours before.

"What do you mean you can't find her? Did you go by her crib?"

"I'm 'bout to step out the door right now and head over there," I told him, grabbing my jacket.

"Give me twenty minutes, and I'll roll with you."

"Thanks, *D.*"

I paced the floor continually, praying the phone would ring and Chrys would be on the other end to tell me she fell asleep. I was filled with anger one moment and frustrated the next. For the life of me, I couldn't figure out what could've happened.

"Hello!" I grabbed the phone before it stopped ringing.

"Hey, Koby." The voice on the other end caused me to cringe.

"Rhea, hey. Look, I don't have time to talk with you right now. I'm 'bout to leave," I said as Dorian walked through my front door.

"Are you going to your mother's for dinner?"

"Yeah, whatever," I said and hung up the phone.

"Was that her?" Dorian asked.

"No. I still can't get in touch with her."

"Let's roll then."

I directed Dorian to Chrys' house. He pulled into the driveway and parked behind her car. "Her car's here, and the lights are on. Maybe you panicked."

"I hope so."

We got out and walked up to the door. I heard footsteps and could see someone looking out the peephole.

I heard her call softly. "Koby?"

"Chrys, are you okay?" I said. "Open the door."

"What are you doing here?"

"I was worried. I've been calling you all night. What's wrong?" I stood back.

"Nothing. I'm fine. I just don't feel well, that's all. I'm sorry I didn't call you."

"Can I come in for a second? I wanna make sure you're okay." I looked at Dorian and shrugged my shoulders.

"No, I'm sorry. I'm not dressed," she said, sniffling.

"Chrys, we're not going anywhere until you open this door!" Dorian yelled.

"Please . . . I'm okay, Dorian. I promise, I will call Koby later."

"Either you open this door right now," Dorian said angrily, "or I am breaking it down! Now try me!"

We heard a click, and the door opened up. Chrys turned her back quickly. "Come in," she said quietly.

We stepped through the doorway and were shocked by what we saw. She was in the midst of cleaning up. The broom and dustpan were leaned against the far wall. What used to be a glass coffee table was shattered in the middle of the floor. A mountain of books was lying around and the bookshelf was bare. The furniture was in disarray, and the lamp had been knocked over.

Dorian looked around. "What the hell . . . ?"

"Chrys, what happened here? Who did this?" I asked.

She sat on the couch, put her hands in her face, and began to cry.

I went over and sat beside her. I reached under her chin and told her to look at me. When she lifted her head, tears came to my eyes. Her eyes were swollen, and her cheek was bruised.

"My God!" Dorian shouted.

"Jesus! Chrys, who did this?" I asked her incredulously.

"My husband." And she buried herself in my chest and cried.

I was stunned. *Married?* I couldn't believe it. *All this time she's been playing me.* Numbness consumed me as I stared at the broken glass lying in the middle of the floor. I could feel the wetness of Chrys' tears through my shirt. For some reason, I couldn't move. All I could think about was the last time I had been played by the woman I was in love with.

Rhea and I had been dating for over a year when she began staying late at the office to work on a big case Michael had coming up. Her birthday was the first week in February, and my birthday fell on Valentine's Day. I decided we both needed a well-deserved break and planned a trip to the Pocono Mountains for her birthday weekend. She called late Thursday afternoon to tell me she couldn't go.

"Rhea, you've been asking me to get away for the weekend for months, and now that I have it all planned for your birthday, you can't go?"

"Baby, you know how important this case is for the firm and my career. I never complain when you have to do research for a class or finish a paper."

"But this is beginning to be a habit. How much longer is this gonna take? I miss you, Rhea."

"I miss you too, Koby. Look, my detailer can't come and pick up my car tomorrow. Can you come and pick it up after work and take it to the place for me?"

"Sure, baby. Better yet, I'll do it myself. I'll give it the Pops Jackson special treatment."

"You are the greatest, Koby—that's why I love you."

"I love you too, Rhea."

After leaving work, I went to meet her in the parking garage where she was waiting with her keys.

She greeted me with a kiss and ran back inside.

I washed and vacuumed the car and put Armor All on the tires. As I was sitting inside to clean the dash, I picked up an ink pen that was lying on the floor. I opened the glove compartment to put it in and noticed some pictures sticking out of some papers. I pulled them out and had to blink twice. There was Rhea, sitting between the legs of Michael Puryear, attorney-at-law, on the sunny beaches of Jamaica, according to what the sign read. His arms were wrapped across her chest, and she had her head lying back on his shoulder. Both of them were smiling as if they were in love. I put the pictures back where I found them, finished the car, and drove back to the parking garage.

Rhea was standing outside when I got there. "Oh, sweetie, it looks so good. My guy never does a job as nice as this."

"No problem. Anything for my girl," I said, trying to sound calm. "How late are you and Michael working tonight?"

"You would not believe how much work he has for me to do. I promise, I won't be working late that much longer though. I will definitely make it up to you on your birthday. You are gonna be my valentine, aren't you?"

"I think Michael would be better suited for that, don't you think?"

Rhea looked at me like I had lost my mind. "Koby, what are you talking about?"

"After all, you did go to Jamaica with him, right?" I stared her in the eye, waiting for her answer.

She took a step back and began shaking her head. "You're crazy, Koby. I don't know who's been lying to you, but you know I haven't been to Jamaica."

"Rhea, don't lie to me, dammit! I saw the pictures." I opened the car door, reached in the glove compartment, and grabbed the pictures. I thrust them in her face. "Where the hell were you in the pictures then, Rhea?—it says *Jamaica*!"

"Koby, those pictures are so old. I can't believe you went snooping through my car. What . . . you don't trust me now?" She snatched the pictures from my hand.

"You really do think I'm stupid? Rhea, the date is printed right on the back—law conference in Boston, my ass!" I looked up and saw Michael watching us from a window.

"Koby, listen to me—" Rhea tried to touch me, but I snatched away.

"I can't believe how stupid I was. Carry your ass back to work, Rhea. You know your boss is waiting!" I stormed across the street to where I'd parked my car. I had never been so angry in my entire life.

I drove around and tried to calm down. I called Dorian on his cell and told him what happened.

"Damn, that's messed up, Koby. I don't blame you for being pissed. You need to just chill out for a minute and get your thoughts together. Hey, let's check out that new Creole place downtown. I heard the food is great." He knew I had a weakness for Cajun cuisine.

"*D*, I really don't feel like going out."

"Yeah, you do. If nothing else, you need a drink."

A few hours later, we were standing outside of the New Orleans-style restaurant about to go in when a couple leaving out caught my eye. They were waiting for the valet to bring their car around and didn't see Dorian and me standing to the side, probably because they were too busy kissing and so wrapped up into each other.

I watched as he traced his fingers down her cheek and she looked into his eyes. He lifted her chin and kissed her. She tiptoed and found his ear, nibbling his lobe, and he closed his eyes.

I walked up to the couple, with Dorian following me. "Good evening, Rhea, Michael."

She gasped. "Koby!"

I reached to shake Michael's hand and introduced him to Dorian. "Michael, this is my best friend, Dorian Silver. Dorian, this is attorney Michael Puryear. I believe you already know Rhea, my *ex*-girlfriend."

Dorian extended his hand to Michael. "Nice to meet you."

"Koby, I can explain."

"Dorian, you ready to go in now? Michael, good to see you again. Rhea, happy birthday." I opened the door, and we entered the restaurant.

That was the last time I saw Rhea, until she showed up at my house the night she attempted to seduce me.

Chapter 9
"Piece of My Love"
—Guy

"Are you sure you don't want to go to the hospital?" Dorian asked gently.

"I'm okay, really. It looks worse than it is." Chrys released her grip from me and wiped the tears from her face.

Dorian pulled his cell from his jacket. "I'm calling the police."

"No!" she shrieked. "I'm sorry. I'm fine, really."

"You need to file a report." Dorian reached down and set up a speaker that had been knocked over.

"Guys, really, I'm fine. You can leave." Chrys sighed and looked around the room.

"We aren't going anywhere until we know you're safe." Dorian began picking up broken glass off the floor.

I got the trash can from the kitchen, and Chrys grabbed the broom. We continued to work in silence.

"Where's your trash?" Dorian asked.

"Through the kitchen and out the back door," she told him. "There's a dumpster to the left."

"You haven't said a word," Chrys said to me while Dorian was gone.

"Sit down, Chrys." I led her to the sofa. "I'm just confused, I guess. I mean, how long have you been married?"

"Two luxurious years. I guess I shoulda said something a long time ago."

"Ya think?" I frowned, my anger growing. "So things got bad between you and you decided to have an affair?"

"I'm not having an affair, Koby."

"Then what the hell do you call this—a fling?— It damn sure ain't a booty call!"

"Oh, is that what this was about? All this time you wanted some booty? Well, I guess I'm a big disappointment for you then? I shoulda known."

"Don't go there." I stood up and began pacing back and forth. "I was the one who shoulda known—I can't believe you've been playing me."

"I haven't been playing you!"

"You're married and ain't say nothing!"

"But he and I aren't together; we're legally separated. My divorce will be final in January. He doesn't even live in this city anymore." She stood up and we squared off, staring at each other intensely.

I could feel myself calming down as I realized what she said. "Oh."

"Yeah, 'oh.' That was one reason for the fight. His family doesn't know that we're separated. He hasn't told them. They don't even know he moved from here. It's Thanksgiving and his family is in town visiting his brother and his fiancée. I am making him look bad. Look how he made me look. Ha, ha, ha." She stood and looked in a mirror that hung on the wall.

"You look beautiful to me." I stood behind her. She did still look beautiful, even with her red, marked face and unkempt hair. Looking at her reflection, I still felt the desire to comfort her, which let me know that, married or not, I still had feelings for her.

"Ahem." Dorian cleared his throat. "Everything all right?"

"Yeah, we're good." I nodded. "You can go ahead and roll, *D*."

"A'ight, man. You sure you gonna be okay?"

"Yeah, we'll be fine," I told him.

He gave Chrys a hug and headed towards the door. I walked him out to his truck. "I'll call you later, *D*."

We dapped each other up and shared a brotherly hug. "You know what you doing, Koby?" he said in my ear. "She's married."

"I'm handling my business the way you told me to."

"I feel ya, bro. Call me if he comes back! I mean it!" Dorian said as he left.

"Now I really feel bad. You don't have to stay here. I told you I'm fine." Chrys began crying again when I returned inside.

I sat beside her and rubbed her back.

"Now what?"

"Now, you go upstairs and pack a bag. I think

you should stay at my place tonight," I told her. I looked at my watch and saw that it was after two in the morning.

"He's not coming back, Koby. I know that."

"That may be so, but I would feel better if you stayed with me for the night."

"Koby—"

"Look . . . either you go with me, or I'm chilling here for the night."

"But—"

"Take your pick."

She stared at the floor for a few moments. "Give me ten minutes."

While she was getting ready, I sat back and tried to absorb everything that had transpired. I was still trying to deal with the fact that Chrys was married. Married . . . and Dorian had me thinking she was a virgin. Suddenly, I was laughing out loud.

"What's so funny?" Chrys asked.

"I'll tell you later." I stood up. "You ready?"

"Yeah, I guess. You really don't have to baby-sit me, Koby."

"Chrys, it's late, I'm tired, and you're driving. This discussion is over. Let's go." I took the small overnight bag out of her hand.

When we got to her car, she paused before getting in.

"What's wrong?"

She just shrugged, unlocked the door, and got in and remained quiet the entire drive to my house. I didn't pressure her to talk because I knew we both were dealing with a lot.

I unlocked the front door to my condo and was

glad that I'd cleaned up earlier in the evening. "Home sweet home."

She looked around my living room. "This is nice."

"You can sleep in my room, and I'll crash down here."

"I don't think so." She sat on my chaise lounge and lay back. "Just get me a blanket, and I'm more than fine right here."

"I'm sure you'll be more comfortable in the bed, Chrys."

She shook her head. "Nope. I'm staying right here." She sat up and reached into her bag, pulled out a scarf, and tied it around her head. "Can I get a blanket?"

"Sure." I walked to the hall closet and grabbed a blanket and a pillow.

"Thanks, Koby, for everything." She spread the blanket over her legs.

I helped tuck her in and placed the pillow behind her head. She touched the side of my face and I leaned into her. Our lips gently met and I inhaled her scent.

"Good night."

"Good night," I whispered.

I was in the middle of making breakfast when she walked into the kitchen Thanksgiving morning.

"I smelled bacon and I thought I was dreaming."

"Good morning. You hungry?"

"Yeah, I am."

"Breakfast'll be ready in a sec," I told her. "You want coffee?"

"Coffee, no, but I would like to take a quick shower first, if that's okay." She rubbed her eyes.

"No problem. Follow me, madam. I'll show you to the throne." I linked my arm into hers and led her up the steps. I had already laid out a washcloth and towel for her.

She looked at me in disbelief. "Koby, you are too much."

"I do aim to please. I gotta get back before my bacon burns. You need anything else?"

"No, you've taken care of everything." She touched the side of her face. "Does it look bad?"

"No, it looks fine." There was a faint mark, but you had to be looking closely to see it. "Hurry before your breakfast gets cold."

By the time Chrys came downstairs, I had pancakes, eggs, bacon and juice laid out on the table and coffee brewing on the counter.

"Wow! I'm impressed."

"What? You ain't know a brother could burn?" I placed a plate of food in front of her.

"From the looks of this bacon, I see you can *burn*."

"Whatever. I like my bacon crunchy," I said, defending my cooking skills.

We sat down and bowed our heads in prayer before eating.

"This is good," she said between bites.

"Hey, I try."

"A man of so many talents."

"Thanks."

The silence between us was agonizing, and we both knew why.

"Okay, you ready to hear my story?" She looked down at her plate.

"If you are ready to tell it."

She looked up briefly. "Where do I begin?"

"Why don't you just start at the beginning?"

"I met my husband about four years ago. I had just graduated and moved here. We were working together at a bank. We started dating and fell in love. He was good to me, and we had what seemed to be a good relationship. We would carpool to work sometimes and have lunch together."

"Sort of like us?"

"Nothing like us; we are different. He's from a so-called prominent family, and he liked to show me off. I had never been wined and dined, so I liked it for a while. But we never really hung out and had fun, like we do. He didn't like to do stuff like that, the arcade and Putt-Putt, you understand?"

"I'm beginning to. Go on."

"One evening, I got off work and my car wouldn't start. He'd already left, so I didn't have a ride. One of the other tellers offered to take me home. She began asking me questions about how we met and how long we had been together. I was naïve and told her all about our relationship. I bragged about how loving he was and how attentive.

"Well, all of a sudden, he felt smothered and felt like he needed some space. The next thing I know, he was taking her to lunch and *they* were carpooling to work."

"Dag!"

"Yeah, my sentiments, exactly. Imagine how I felt having to work with the both of them. I immediately searched for employment elsewhere. That's when I got hired at the phone company three years ago.

"After I moved here and we were apart for a minute, I guess you could say we reconciled and married a year later. He quit his job and moved here with me. Then he started hanging out at night. Soon after we were married, I got suspicious . . . women's intuition—I think that's what they call it. I began to check his pager."

"Did you call the numbers back?"

"No, you don't get it. I figured out the pass code and listened to the messages."

"Wow! What did you hear?"

She got up from the table and went into the living room. She came back with a small tape recorder.

"You taped 'em?"

"Listen." She pressed *play*.

I'm sorry I am unable to take your call right now. Leave your name and number, and I'll get back, a deep voice said.

Beep—Hey, teddy bear, this is Chevay. I just called to say good morning after the night we had last night. Umm, thank you and please cum again. Call me when you get this.

Beep—Hey, baby, this is Lori. I am really trying to see you tonight so we can finish what we started. Please call me and make my day.

Beep—Hi, sexy, this is Darla. You didn't call me like

you said you would. I miss you and can't wait to put my mouth where it hasn't been in a while . . . and you know how you like when I do that. Let me know what time you're coming by so I can be ready for ya.

She clicked off the recorder and sat down. "That was during our third month of marriage. Imagine how I felt, a new bride; we were still supposed to be in the honeymoon stage. Then he started drinking heavily. I must've been a terrible wife, huh?"

"No, he was just an immature bastard. So what happened?"

"He got physical with me one night—I packed my stuff the next day and I left."

"So he's done this before?"

"Not really. Only once. The first time he hit me, I left him. For me, that was all it took. Last night, it got bad because I fought back. That's why the table is broken—I pushed him through it."

"'Fought back,' huh?"

"Yep, he was in my house and I wasn't trying to have it."

"How do you know he's not coming back?"

"I know him. He's probably lying to his family that I cheated on him to make me look like a tramp."

"You could never be a tramp."

"Thanks. They wouldn't think so. Whatever he says, goes. It's my fault though."

"How could you think that? Why?"

"I knew he was trifling before I married him and still went through with it."

"We've all made mistakes in love." I thought about my own relationship woes.

The phone rang, startling both of us. I got up from the table to answer it. "Hello."

"Koby, Mama said pick up a bag of ice on your way over here," Jaamell said, chewing in my ear.

"Jaamell, how about saying hello first." I shook my head. "And stop chewing in my ear!"

"My bad. Hello, Mama said bring some ice." He smacked his lips.

"You are so ignorant, it's hard to believe we have the same mother and father."

"Whatever. Just bring the ice. I gotta go—she's taking the ham out the oven now."

I hung the phone up and looked over at Chryslin, who was grinning at me. "My little brother . . . we're still in the process of teaching him telephone etiquette."

"I bet the two of you are so cute going back and forth," she said.

"I guess you'll have a front row seat in a little while. Come on, we need to get ready."

She looked puzzled. "Get ready for what?"

"You have fifteen minutes."

"Where am I going?"

"Uh, it's Thanksgiving, remember? We have to get going to the crib so we can eat. Now you only have fourteen minutes. You'd better hurry, or I'm leaving you."

"This early?"

"It's not early; it's already after ten." I cleared the table and put the dirty dishes in the sink.

"I really don't feel up to going. You go and be with your family."

"Don't even try it." I pulled her up out of the chair. "You are my family. Now go!" I pushed her out of the kitchen and playfully swatted her on the behind.

Chapter 10
"I Wanna Know"

—Joe

Thanksgiving dinner was one of the best we ever had. Momma and Jackie really outdid themselves with the meal, and my family welcomed Chrys with open arms. No one mentioned her eye. Dorian told my parents that Chrys had an accident, but told Jackie the truth. Even Jaamell's new girlfriend, Chela made Chrys feel good by mentioning how beautiful she was.

Chrys blushed. "Thank you."

Pop said, "She sure is—now you know Theodore and I teach driving school if you need us—"

"Pop!" I was so embarrassed.

We were all sitting in the den listening to some of Pop's old albums, while he and Uncle Theodore talked about their latest business ideas.

The doorbell rang, and Jaamell went to answer it.

"Hey, Pops, that just might work," Dorian said.

Jaamell called and told me, "Come here."

"What, Jaamell?"

"Come here!"

"No—*you* come here!" I yelled back to the amusement of everyone.

A familiar voice rang out. "I'll go see him myself. I know the way!"

My heart began beating so fast. I almost couldn't catch my breath. I jumped up and headed out of the den, but she was in the doorway before I could make it.

"Happy Thanksgiving, everyone!" she sang.

Momma, Pops, Dorian, Jackie, Chela, and the kids all looked at me with their mouths hanging open. No one moved.

Chrys looked at Rhea. "Happy Thanksgiving to you."

"Hello, Rhea," Momma finally said.

"Mother Jackson, how have you been?" She walked over to my mother and gave her a hug.

"What are you doing here, Rhea?" I asked, trying to remain calm.

"Yes—why are you here?—It certainly didn't come by invitation," Jackie tried to get up, but Dorian grabbed her arm.

"It's Thanksgiving. And when I called Koby last night, he suggested I come by."

"No, I didn't. You asked if I was coming over here. I don't even remember answering you."

Jackie glared at her. "And you took *that* as an invitation?"

"Dorian, I'm so glad to see you. I've been meaning to call so I can finally get my Lexus." Rhea looked at Chrys. "And you are?"

Chrys smiled at her. "I'm Chryslin—an invited guest."

Rhea gave Chrys a menacing look and turned around. "Look at the babies . . . they are getting so big!"

That definitely got to Jackie. She grabbed Chrys and told her to come out and get some air.

I scowled. "Rhea, why are you here?"

"I came by to see you and your family. I miss you and I want to talk to you, Koby."

Pops suggested, "Koby, why don't you and Rhea go talk in the living room?"

"Sure, Pop." I led Rhea out of the den.

"Was that your date? Is that why you haven't had time for me? Because of Kristen?"

"*Chryslin* is my friend. And I don't have time for you because I choose not to have time for you."

"Look, Koby, I just want to ask you to forgive me. I was wrong and I disrespected you and our relationship, but more importantly, I disrespected our friendship. I am sorry because that friendship is important to me and you are important to me." Rhea was crying through all of this. "Koby, I was stupid and I took you for granted. Please . . . all I want is your forgiveness and for you to tell me that we can at least be friends."

I stood back and folded my arms. "Rhea . . . look, now is not the right time for us to be having this discussion. It's Thanksgiving and I'm trying to spend time with my family. You show up uninvited and unannounced and you think I'm gonna talk to you about being my friend?"

"I know, but I didn't know what else to do. I call

you and you brush me off, I come to your house and you throw me out. I just want you to forgive me, Koby . . . please."

"Come on, Rhea. Look . . . even though things didn't work out the way we expected them to, we had some good times and we have some great memories—you know that."

"Then how can you stand there and act like I don't mean anything to you, Koby? . . . because that's how you make me feel—like nothing."

I looked into her pleading eyes and saw that she was being sincere. "Rhea, I forgave you a while ago, but that doesn't mean I forgot."

"I don't expect you to forget, Koby, and I can see that you've moved on. I just need to know that one day, even if it's not today, that somehow we can be friends."

I shrugged. "Okay, Rhea, we're cool."

A smile spread across her face. "Thanks, Koby. Well, I guess I crashed the party. I'll go apologize to your parents and be on my way." She walked back into the den and spoke briefly to my parents.

When she came back out, she asked, "Can a sister get some peach cobbler and a piece of pound cake for the road?"

"Sure," I told her, "I'll get it for you."

While I was making her plate, Chrys and Jackie came through the back door. "I know you ain't fixin' that heifer no plate?" Jackie said loudly.

"Chill, Jackie. It's a to-go plate. It's Thanksgiving. She can get some cake, can't she?"

"Why can't she get some cake from Michael's momma's house?—she was getting everything else from Michael! See, Chrys, this girl causes me to get ghetto. Now you know I usually don't act like this."

Chrys stood next to the counter giggling.

"Shut up, Jackie!" I said laughing. "You are one cold-blooded sister." I looked at Chrys. "And why are you laughing?"

Before Chrys could answer, Jackie said, "Because it's funny!"

Chrys laughed even harder.

I finished wrapping the plate and took it out to Rhea, who was talking to Jaamell and Chela. "Here you go!" I handed her the plate.

"Thanks, Koby. Well, it was nice meeting you, Chela. And Jaamell . . . call me about that summer job with the firm."

"No problem. Thanks for the hook-up, Rhea." Jaamell gave her a hug.

I looked at him like he was crazy. He looked at me and shrugged, and he and Chela went back into the den.

I asked her, "What was that about?"

"He told me he wanted a summer job, and I told him I'd try to get him one with the firm," she said innocently.

"And are you going to make the hour drive to pick him up and take him home every day?"

"He can stay with you for the summer. It's a great opportunity for him; it'll look good on his college applications. His girlfriend is so pretty. By the way, is it serious between you and *Chryslin*?"

"None of your business, Rhea. Come on, I'll walk you out to your car."

She turned to me before getting into her car. "Can I call you every now and then? . . . just to talk, that's all."

"Sure." I gave her a quick hug and turned to go back into the house.

"She is beautiful. Is she a model?" Chrys said later that night as we headed home.

"No. And her beauty is nothing compared to yours." I grabbed her hand.

"Yes, I've heard that a bruised face does have that sensual appeal." She giggled.

"No one even noticed the bruise."

"That's because I worked my magic with the makeup." She pulled the vanity mirror down and looked at her face.

"You shoulda left it uncovered. Truth be told, I was turned on by it. Looks like a sexy birthmark." I laughed as we pulled up to my house.

We got out and walked up to my door.

"Yeah, right. I know. All day you've been think-ing, 'Damn! She is sexy. I just want to take her and—'"

Before she could finish, I pulled her to me and covered her mouth with mine. Her eyes were wide with surprise for a moment, and then she relaxed. Her full lips opened, and I tasted her soft tongue touching mine. I could feel her hands behind my head pulling me closer as I cupped her face with my hands. Our mouths searched each other's.

I was moaning now. My heart began beating faster as we kissed and nibbled harder. After what seemed like hours, we finally broke away. I looked deep into her eyes. "That is what I've been thinking since the first day I met you."

"Great minds think alike. Now what?"

"Now we go inside."

"And?"

"And whatever you want . . ."

Tears began to form in her eyes. "Whatever I want?"

"What's wrong?"

"I don't know. It's just that most guys, if they would've found out I was married and beat up at that . . . and here you are telling me it's about what I want." Tears rolled down her cheeks.

"Hey, I'm not 'most guys.'" I wiped her tears away with my thumb and kissed her gently.

"If you treated her this nice and she messed it up, then her loss is my gain." She smiled.

"And the best woman will win!" I said as we entered my house.

"Your parents are so nice, and your little brother and his girlfriend are cute." Chrys took her coat off. "What color are his eyes?"

"Grey. He got them from my grandmother." I took mine off and hung both of them in the closet.

"I guess that gene passed you up, huh?" She looked at me and smiled.

"Yeah," I said as I sat on the sofa, "but I got all of the other good qualities."

"Really? And what qualities are those?"

"Oh . . . charm, wit, intelligence, brilliance—" I pulled her into my lap.

She fell on top of me, laughing. "Now don't be modest."

I held her close, inhaling her scent, and rubbing my hand across her back.

"What time is it?" she asked.

"Almost ten—why?"

"I gotta call my mom. Can you pass me my phone?"

"Yeah." I reached over and passed her the phone that was attached to her purse.

She dialed a series of numbers and put the phone to her ear. "Hello. Hi, Ma, Happy Thanksgiving. I tried calling you earlier, but you weren't home. I don't know why you don't get a cell phone; I'll pay for it, Mama. Jeez . . . Yeah, it was great . . . Really? No—she did what?" She laughed heartily. "And what did Uncle Johnnie say? . . . I bet she was mad. Okay, Ma, I'll call you later this weekend . . . I love you too." She clicked the phone off and lay back in my lap.

"Your family okay?"

"Yeah. I miss them. It's hard being so far from home . . . especially during the holidays. When I moved up here, all I was thinking about was getting away from my ex and making a new start; it seemed to make sense at the time. I didn't realize what I was leaving behind. You're lucky to have your family so close." She sighed and stared into the blank television screen. "Where's the remote?"

I reached on the coffee table and gave it to her.

She flipped through the channels and stopped at the opening credits to *The Wiz* as I held her in my arms.

Soon we drifted into sleep as Dorothy, Toto, the Tin Man, and the Lion tried to find their way home.

Chapter 11

"Kissing You"

—Faith Evans

Chrys and I met up with Dorian and Jackie the next morning for brunch and some shopping. Since their kids were with Momma, we decided to make it a mini-vacation weekend. We hit the highway and drove four hours to one of the largest outlet cities on the East Coast. We went in and out of stores, laughing and buying gifts all day Friday. We even took the time to try on jewelry in an exclusive store on a dare by Dorian.

When dusk came, we decided to check into the hotel and rest a bit before meeting for dinner. I used the key card and let Chrys into the room.

"I have never had so much fun in my entire life!" she said.

"My sentiments, exactly. Boy, I am tired." I stretched.

Chrys walked over and put her arms around my waist.

"Well, I am gonna take a shower first." She rubbed her head against my shoulder.

"Need any help? I can wash your back."

"No, thanks. I got it. I know backwashing is one of those great qualities you inherited from your grandmother, right?" She opened her suitcase.

"But, of course." I hugged her from behind.

I fell asleep while she was showering. As I tried to turn, I felt her curled up beside me. I looked at her angelic face. *I could wake up every morning exactly like this.*

Although we had kissed on several occasions, we had never gotten any further. I didn't push the issue, deciding to let things happen naturally. Chrys was so special, and something told me she would definitely be worth the wait. Sleeping in the same bed with her beside me the entire weekend without making love to her was going to be the hardest thing I'd ever had to do.

She stirred under my arm. "Hey," she said smiling.

"Hey, yourself. Did you sleep okay?"

"Great! What time is it?"

"Time to get up and get ready. Jackie and Dorian will be calling in a minute, and if we aren't ready they will be banging on the door."

We got up and quickly dressed in time to hear a knock at the door.

"Now, do you see why it's important to be early." She grabbed my hand and we joined them in the hallway.

* * *

The remainder of the weekend was just as fun and relaxing as the first day. I hated to see Sunday evening come.

We pulled into my driveway. I sat in the car, not wanting to get out. "Why don't you stay the night?" I asked her.

She laughed. "Because I have to go home— aren't you sick of me? We've been together like four days straight."

"No, I could never get sick of you; I'm sick when I'm *not* with you."

"Come on, I've got to get ready for tomorrow. We do have jobs, remember?"

"We can car pool; you can ride with me. Please? . . . Just one more night?"

"No. Come on, you can help me with my bags."

I popped the trunk, walked around to the back of the car, and reluctantly got the bags out.

"Well, I guess I'll see you tomorrow." She unlocked her car and put her bags into the back seat.

"Maybe I should stay with you tonight . . . in case he comes back."

"He's not coming back, but if he does, I promise, I will call you. Better yet, I'll jump in the car and drive over here."

"No."

"'No'? Why not?"

I said, "Because I don't want you to leave," and kissed her full on the mouth.

Chrys responded by grabbing the back of my head and pulling me in closer. She tastily began to suck on my bottom lip and gently stroked my neck.

"Okay, I really gotta go." She nuzzled her head against my chin. "But there is something I've gotta say before I leave."

"What is it?"

"I want to thank you for a wonderful weekend. You have been my knight in shining armor from the moment I met you. You are a true gentleman and show me nothing but respect. Not one time did you do or suggest anything inappropriate, and as much as I want to stay, I just don't think I have the willpower to not do anything that I know both you and I want to do. Do you understand what I am trying to say?"

"Not really. Because if it's something we both want, then I don't see anything wrong. Lord knows, I want you . . . in more ways than one." I cupped her face in my hands and looked into her eyes. "Please . . . just stay the night with me."

"Not tonight, Koby," she whispered.

I was beyond aroused. I wanted to scoop Chrys into my arms, take her inside, and do things to her that she probably never imagined. I wanted her so much that standing there in front of her was making me frustrated.

She stepped away from me and opened her car door. "Koby?" She got in and started the engine.

"Yeah." I sighed.

"I'll call you when I get home." She gazed at me. "I love you."

Chapter 12

"Your Body's Calling"

—R. Kelly

I had big plans for Chrys' birthday the following weekend. She and I really hadn't spent a lot of quality time together since Thanksgiving. We saw each other in passing at work and continued our late-night phone conversations, but I couldn't wait to wake up with her in my arms after a night of passionate lovemaking that I knew was soon to come.

I called her at precisely midnight on her birthday. "Happy birthday, baby. You want me to come over?"

"Thank you so much for the offer, but I can wait."

"But I want to give you your birthday hug."

"Later."

"And your birthday kiss."

"Later."

"And your birthday licks."

"'Licks'? Lick where?" she said seductively.

"Well, I was talking about *spanking*, but now that you have my attention, where would you like me to lick?"

"Oh no—you tell me where *you* want to lick me."

"It's *your* birthday. You can pick wherever it is."

"Well, let's start with my neck."

"That's a good place to start."

"And let's see, there's my collar . . . ooh . . ."

"Uh-huh, keep going."

"How about my chest?"

"How about your *breast?*—that's more like it." I sat up in the bed.

"Okay." She giggled. "Now, how about my . . . hand."

"Your *hand?*"

"Uh-huh, the palm of my hand."

I could hear her breathing getting heavy through the phone. "Oh, okay. And then I get to suck your fingers—one by one."

"Ooh, that sounds really good."

"And nibble your arms and shoulders." I was really beginning to get turned on. I had to reposition myself in the bed. "And lick down the center of your back."

"And kiss my thighs."

"Yeah, and then spread them open." I put my hand in my sweats.

"Um, and then . . ."

I began rubbing myself harder. "And then what?"

"Then you eat my birthday cake." She laughed.

"And lick all the icing off?" I whispered.

"Yep, 'cuz it's so sweet." She moaned through the phone. "Koby?"

"Yeah, boo?"

"Do I get to lick your ice-cream?" She laughed hysterically.

I couldn't help joining her. "You really know how to spoil a moment, don't you?" I said.

"Good night, Koby. See you tomorrow."

"Good night, baby. Happy birthday."

The next morning I woke in anticipation of what the day had in store. And more importantly, the night. I knew that Chrys' team at work would be having a party for her during lunch and decided to have twenty-seven roses delivered to her desk: a dozen white, for romance; a dozen pink, for affection; two yellow, for friendship; and a single red one, for love.

The card read:

> *To Chrys,*
> *Your driving skills were oh so bad,*
> *And into me you had to crash.*
> *And although you severely damaged my ride,*
> *At least now I have you by my side.*
> *Happy Birthday with Love,*
> *Koby*

That afternoon, I received a message on my phone:

> *They are beautiful! Thank you so much!*
> *And my heart you know they touched!*

You know I can drive, quit being a hater.
Don't forget about cake and ice-cream later (hint, hint).

I had a wonderful evening planned for Chrys. I told her I would be picking her up precisely at 6:30.

I had reserved a private table for two on the dinner cruise at the harbor. I'd also reserved a hotel room with a balcony, at the Marriott. When we arrived in the room, there would be champagne and chocolate-dipped strawberries waiting for us. In addition, Jackie had gone over earlier to set up candles and massage oil.

I got home from work in record time. My clothes were already laid out, so I only had to shower and shave. The Giorgio Armani suit I had been saving for an occasion such as this, fit perfect on my 6-2, 245-pound frame.

I had gotten my hair cut and face trimmed professionally the day before, but touched it up myself nonetheless. I decided to keep it old-school, and chose Drakkar as my fragrance for the night.

I slid into my shoes, grabbed my overnight bag. I was headed down the steps, when I heard the doorbell ring. I checked my watch and noticed it was 6:00. *Right on time.*

"Mr. Jackson?" the man in the dark suit asked.

"Yes, just give me one second and I'll be right out."

"Yes, sir." He turned and headed down the walkway.

I double-checked my bag and made sure I had

the CD I made. I grabbed the silver foil-wrapped gifts off the coffee table and locked the door as I left out.

I gave the driver directions.

When we pulled in front of Chrys' house. I got out and took a deep breath. I walked to her door and rang the doorbell.

"Happy birthday, baby!"

"Thank you! Right on time, I see." She greeted me with a kiss.

I grinned. "I learned from the best."

She had on a black overcoat, so I couldn't tell what she had on. I could still admire those fabulous legs though. Her face was madeup to perfection, and I inhaled Escada as she brushed past me to get her purse.

I asked her, "You got your overnight bag?"

"Yeah, right there." She pointed to the black Coach duffel bag on the sofa—"Nothing. You ready?"

"Let's roll." I grabbed the bag and her hand and led her out the door.

"Oh my God! A limo! Koby . . ." She stopped dead in her tracks.

"Hey, you only turn twenty-seven once. Now, come on, we're gonna be late." I pulled her towards the car. The driver opened the door, and we got in.

She screamed again after getting in and seeing the back of the limo filled with silver and white balloons. "Are you ever going to stop amazing me?" She said with tears in her eyes.

"I hope not." I gave her a small silver-wrapped box. "Madame, gift number one. Open."

"Gift number one was the phone call this morning. And gift number two was the roses, gift number three is this limo—"

"Can you please just open the gift?"

She carefully unwrapped the small box that held a Blackberry phone that she wanted. "Thank you so much, Koby!" She gave me a passionate kiss.

"Wow! If that's what I get for a Blackberry, then hurry up and open the next gift!" I passed her the large foil-wrapped box.

This time she just ripped it open and screeched with glee.

I once asked Chrys what was the one thing she always wanted and never got. When she told me, I didn't hesitate getting her one for her birthday.

"Ah, a George Foreman grill! Thank you, thank you, thank you!" She smothered my face with kisses.

"I take it you like your gifts?" I grinned at her.

"This is the best birthday ever!"

"And this is just beginning." I pulled her close to me.

"Where are we going, Koby?"

"I told you—to dinner."

We pulled into the harbor where they had just begun to board the boat. The driver helped us out, and we were led to our intimate table by the porter.

I helped Chrys remove her coat. My eyes widened with excitement, when I saw the form-fitting black dress she had on. Her ample cleavage drew my attention, and she took notice. "You like?"

"No, I *love*."

"You are a trip." She laughed and hugged me, and I caressed her neck.

* * *

Dinner was lovely. The cruise had a DJ that played a mixture of hits and we danced and laughed until I suggested we go up to the deck.

We stepped outside and were greeted by a star-filled night. Chrys shivered in the brisk air. I took off my jacket and wrapped it around her arms.

"I don't know what I did to deserve this." She leaned into my arms.

"I don't either, but it must've been good."

"You are so funny."

As she turned to me, my mouth met hers, and our tongues found each other again, dancing like two old friends who hadn't seen each other in years. I put my hands under my jacket and rubbed her arms, which she had wrapped around my waist. She rubbed her nose against mine, and we looked deep into each other's eyes.

I saw the tears begin to form in her eyes and tilted my head. "I hope those are tears of happiness," I told her.

"You can't imagine."

The boat pulled back into the harbor, and the limo met us. We snuggled all the way to the hotel. After the driver pulled into the circular driveway and opened the door for us to get out, I got our bags and the gifts out, and tipped him.

I turned to Chrys. "Ready?"

"Yeah, but how are we gonna get home?"

"My car is in the hotel parking garage. Dorian dropped it off for me."

"Oh, okay. You want me to wait while you pull around?"

"You don't want to spend the night?"

"We're staying here?"

"What? Please don't front like you didn't know, now come on!"

We entered the lobby of the hotel.

"If I told you I wasn't ready, would you be mad?" she asked as we rode the elevator.

"Nope."

"Not even a little bit?"

I touched her cheek. "Not even a little bit."

I used the card and we entered the room, which followed the silver and white theme of the evening— balloons, candles, and a foil sign hung overhead, which read "Happy Birthday, Chrys."

She gasped as she walked in. "Wow!"

"You like?"

"I love."

I popped open the bottle of champagne, which was chilling on the small coffee table. I poured each of us a glass and walked over to Chrys who sat on the side of the bed and was taking off her shoes. "Toast," I said as I gave her the flute. She began to raise her glass to mine, and I yelled out, "Wait."

I reached inside my duffel bag and found my CD organizer. I flipped through, removed the disc I was searching for, and placed into the player. "Don't drink yet!"

"What are you doing?"

I reached into the refrigerator, removed the silver platter with chocolate-dipped strawberries, and brought them over to the bed. I pulled her up and faced her. I licked the end of the berry and then placed it seductively into her mouth.

"Umm . . . juicy." She licked her lips and smiled at me. "What happened to the music?"

"Oh, just a minute." I ran over to the player and hit the play button. I bobbed my head to the beat of the Isley Brothers' "For the Love of You."

She smiled. "Are you trying to seduce me?"

"Of course not. Now, a toast—to Chrys, the most beautiful woman I have ever had the pleasure of courting, may we continue to grow in this relationship and surpass anything you and I ever thought we could be. Happy birthday."

"Here, here!"

We touched glasses, and I wrapped my arms around her and kissed her. We began to sway to the music, and my body began to yearn for hers. I looked deep into her eyes and asked her, "You ready for ice- cream?"

"Funny . . . I was about to ask you if you wanted some cake."

I nodded and slowly led her to the bed, where she sat on the edge. "You sure about this?" I asked her.

She pulled me down on top of her, looked into my eyes, and kissed me deeply. She began to un-button my shirt.

I began kissing her neck as she arched her back. I reached and unzipped the back of her dress to reveal her full breasts enclosed in a black lace bra.

She began to moan as I rubbed her nipples through the sexy material. She maneuvered out of the dress, and it fell to the floor.

I raised myself off the bed and stood back.

"What? What's wrong?" She looked alarmed.

"God, you are beautiful," I said, admiring her firm body. She looked perfect to me. I looked at her from head to toe for what seemed like an eternity. Her nipples were fully aroused and at full attention. I took notice of her sexy black garter with matching thong underneath and smiled. "My kind of girl."

"My kind of guy." She said as she removed my shirt completely and licked my chest. Her hands undid my pants, and I stepped out of them as they fell to my ankles. She wrapped her perfectly manicured fingers around me and growled seductively, "Definitely, my kind of man."

"I do aim to please." I unhooked her bra and kneeled down in front of her.

She tossed her head back in amusement, and as she did so I spread her legs wide. I removed her stockings one by one and kissed each of her feet, trailing a line along the back of her calf with my tongue. I could feel her gasp, as I nibbled her inner thighs and my mouth worked its way up. "Now, is this the cake I've been waiting to eat?" I asked as my fingers spread her wetness open. I placed my head between her legs and inhaled her scent. "Chocolate . . . my favorite," I said and savored her. I could feel her shudder as my tongue plunged deeper.

"Oh, Koby!" Chrys cried as she climaxed.

I raised myself up to her and smiled. "Did I get all the icing?"

"You licked the platter clean, baby," she said as she caught her breath and kissed me.

Making love to Chrys was incredible. I had

never felt so satisfied in my life. It was as if our bodies were made for each other and we couldn't get enough.

Definitely worth the wait, I thought as I woke up with her in my arms.

Chapter 13

"I Believe in You and Me"

—Whitney Houston

The wind whipped against my ears as I ran towards the front entrance of the mall. *I gotta get me a hat*, I thought as the doors opened. Momma had dropped Jaamell and Chela off earlier, and we were meeting Chrys for some last-minute shopping.

I caught the escalator and spotted Chrys in front of Foot Locker. "Hey, sweetie." I greeted her with a kiss.

"Hey," she said, "Jaamell and Chela are trying on shoes."

"Typical. It's the season for giving and they are out shopping for themselves." I shook my head as I watched Jaamell stand and pose in the Jordans he had on his feet.

"They may be shopping for each other. Come on, scrooge"—She grabbed my hand and led me inside the store.

Jaamell greeted me with a smile. "Koby, what's up?"

I gave Jaamell a pound—"Hey, *J*"—and hugged Chela. "How ya doing, Ms. Chela?"

"You like these, Koby?" he asked me.

"Yeah, *J*. They are all right."

He turned to Chela. "What you think, Che?"

"They look good on your feet, Jaamell; I like them."

"Man, I've gotta come back and get these after Christmas. Girl, you'd better be glad I love you." He looked at Chela.

Chrys hit me on my arm as we watched him slowly give the shoes to the salesman. "I told you," she whispered, "he was just trying them on."

As we exited the store, I asked him, "Who all do you have to shop for, *J*?"

"You, Momma, Pop, Mookie, Dor—"

Chrys interrupted him. "Okay, who have you shopped for?"

He blushed. "Chela."

I asked him, "You mean Christmas is three days away and you've only bought one gift?"

Chela wrapped her arms around his waist. "Leave him alone."

"And who have you shopped for?" I asked Chela.

She looked at us with a bashful smile. "Jaamell."

"Why am I not surprised?" I said to Chrys. "Well, it looks like we have a lot to do, guys. Everybody ready? Let's hit it." I grabbed Chrys' hand.

Little did they know, the only gift I had purchased was Dorian's. And that was because I noticed him looking at a particular cigar humidor when we were at the outlet; I went back and got it without his knowing. I hadn't even gotten Chrys' gift yet. I figured I'd notice her admiring something and get it the same way I got Dorian's—without her even knowing it.

For the remainder of the afternoon, we went in and out of the stores, laughing and joking. By the time the mall was closing, I had gotten the majority of my shopping done.

As we were getting ready to leave, Chrys stopped at a jewelry showcase to look at a beautiful pair of diamond earrings with a matching pendant. "What do you think of these?" she asked, when I walked up behind her and put my arms around her.

"Those are the bomb, as Jaamell would say. They are gorgeous."

"I'm thinking about getting them." She tilted her head and looked at me.

"I love them," I said as we leaned against the window.

"Man, I am hungry," I heard Jaamell say to Chela as they walked past.

"I guess we need to feed them, huh?" I turned and looked into her beautiful eyes.

"Yep, you need to feed me too."

"Really?" I said slyly. "You want some ice-cream?"

She smiled and shook her head at me. "You are so nasty."

"Man, try to give you something sweet and this is the thanks I get." I kissed her.

"Uh, do you think that can wait until you get home?" Jaamell yelled to us.

"And what car are you driving, Jaamell?" I yelled back.

Chela giggled as we headed out of the mall.

We trailed Chrys to her house to drop off her car. There was a bouquet of flowers waiting on her doorstep. She gestured for me to wait a moment and read the card as she was opening the door. She came out soon after and got into the car.

"Flowers?" I asked.

"Belated birthday."

"Must be nice to have a birthday and then turn right around and have Christmas," Jaamell commented from the back seat.

"Not really," she said. "I either get really good birthday gifts *or* really good Christmas gifts."

"Same here," I told her. "Being born on Valentine's Day is no fun either."

"Poor baby. Tell you what, I promise this year you'll get a Valentine's Day gift *and* a birthday gift." She leaned over to give me a kiss.

"I just want some cake!" I grinned knowingly and kissed her back.

"Get a room!" Jaamell groaned.

We stopped at Applebee's and grabbed a quick dinner and then headed to take Jaamell and Chela home. The drive went by quickly due to Chrys and Chela deciding we should sing carols.

By the time we pulled into the driveway, Jaamell and I both breathed a sigh of relief. We grabbed his and Chela's bags out of the trunk and helped them carry them into the house.

"Ooh, looks like someone went and found Santa," Momma said as we walked in. She tried to take one of the bags from Jaamell.

He stopped her instantly. "No peeking, Ma!"

"Don't do that, Jenny!" Pop said as he came into

the foyer. "Let me help you with those, son." He reached for the bags.

Jaamell snatched them back. "Stop playing, Pop! Chela, can you grab some of these for me?"

They went to hide the packages in Jaamell's room while we stood in the foyer, laughing.

"Well, we are gonna get going," I told my parents.

"Thanks so much for bringing them home for me," Momma said.

"It was fun. I really enjoyed them." Chrys hugged Momma and Pop as we got ready to leave.

"We will see you all Christmas morning at Dorian's." Pop opened the door and walked us out. "Theodore and I plan on—"

Momma pulled Pop into the house. "Bye, Koby and Chrys! Love you!"

As we got on the highway, Chrys asked, "Are you sleepy? I can drive if you need me to."

"Uh, I don't think so—I mean, no, babe, I'm fine." I grabbed her hand.

She gave me a fake evil look. "Whatever." She leaned over and whispered in my ear. "Well, let me at least help you stay awake."

"Ooh . . . I like the sound of that. What are you gonna do to keep me up?"

She leaned all the way over and placed her hand on my thigh. "I'm gonna tell you what I saw . . . last night." She moved her hand farther up my leg.

"What was that?" I was getting aroused as she rubbed my crotch.

She sang loudly, "*I saw mommy kissing Santa Claus . . .*"

"Come on, man!"

*   *   *

"Are you coming in?" she asked when we got to her house.

"Are you inviting me in?"

"Come on, silly."

We went into her house and she hung our jackets up. I noticed the flowers from earlier sitting on the kitchen table. I kicked off my Tims and sat on her chaise lounge.

She walked over and sat between my legs as she clicked on the TV. "Ooh . . . *The Bodyguard*!" she squealed.

I grabbed the remote and quickly changed the channel. "Oh, no, I am not watching this!"

"Please . . . come on, it's good."

"Nope." I kept flipping. "Oh, snap! This is my movie."

"*A Christmas Story*!" she whined. "It comes on every day this month!"

I grinned. "I know!"

She teased, "'But, Ralphie, you'll shoot your eye out!'" and tried to grab the remote from me.

We sat back and watched the movie for a while.

"Are you sleepy?" I asked her, rubbing her neck.

"Yeah, are you?" She tilted her head back.

I let my hands drift across her chest and palmed her breasts. "Yeah. I guess I need to be going."

She lifted her hand to my mouth and kissed it. "You're not staying?"

"You want me to?" I kissed her neck.

"Don't front like you don't want to," she said and turned to face me. She placed my fingers in her mouth, one at a time and sucked them.

I felt a sensation go down my spine. "How bad you want me to stay?" I removed her shirt.

"Let me show you." She took her hair out of the ponytail and it fell to her shoulders. She removed her jeans and revealed her red, holly-covered underwear.

"Cute." I smiled at her.

"I figured you'd appreciate them." She lifted my shirt over my head and kissed my chest. She licked my body lower, and lower, until she got to the top of my jeans. She unbuttoned them, reached in with her hand, and wrapped her fingers around my growing manhood. She pulled my jeans off and got on her knees. She looked up at me and seductively asked, "Can I have my ice-cream now?"

"Every last drop, baby. Every last drop."

Chapter 14

"How Deep Is Your Love"

—Keith Sweat

I thought I was dreaming when I heard the phone ringing early the next morning. I opened my eyes and had to remember where I was.

I heard Chrys talking inside the bathroom. "Yeah, I got them. Thanks . . . No, I don't think that's a good idea . . . Well, congratulations to him . . . No . . . Yes . . . I know . . . I promise. This isn't easy for me either. You too. Talk to you later. Bye."

I closed my eyes and pretended to be asleep as she climbed back into bed. "Just relax," I told myself. "Breathe."

She wrapped her arms around me and pulled her body close to mine.

"Koby," she whispered, "you asleep?"

"No." I reached and put my hand on her thigh. "What time is it?"

"After ten. You want me to cook you breakfast?"

"No, I'm good—so what was that all about?"

"What?"

"Don't play, you know what—the phone call in the bathroom."

"It was nothing," she said. "Not even worth talking about. Really."

"Okay, if you say so. What do you want to do today?"

"I have to get my hair done this afternoon and finish my shopping."

"Oh."

"You want to hook up later this evening?"

"That's cool. Come on, let's get up."

"Right now? Let's stay here a little while longer." She snuggled closer to me and rubbed my chest with her fingers.

I told her, "I could stay here with you forever," and put my hands over hers.

"I can't believe I am having an affair," she said quietly.

"Not really; you're separated. No longer together."

"But I am not divorced."

I turned to look her. "Are you having regrets?"

"Regrets about getting married, yes; regrets about you, no. Sometimes I think about the fact that I made a vow and I broke it. I try not to dwell on it."

I could see the tears forming in her eyes. "Do you want me to give you some space . . . until you think this out?"

"No, I am fine."

"You're not fine, Chrys. I just don't want you to look back on all of this and think we rushed into something you didn't want to do."

"Koby, you are the best thing to ever happen in my life. Believe me, if that were not true, I would've never gone out with you in the first place. Honestly, you are only the second man I have ever been with in my life." She looked away, blushing.

"You mean—"

"That's right—I was a virgin when I met my husband. I told you, he was my first love in every way possible, but he took advantage of that position and I can't deal with that."

"I gotta ask you a question. We said we were gonna be open and honest, right?"

"Yep."

"The flowers?"

"They weren't from him; those were from his mom."

"And the phone call earlier was nothing?"

"No, that was his father, who happens to be a minister. I've been separated for almost a year, but he just told them on Thanksgiving. As you can see, his family isn't taking it very well. But, I cannot deal with him or his crap any longer. It's over, and all of them need to get over it . . . I mean that. Life is too short to keep winding up hurt by the same person; I am determined to not let that happen again."

"Well, I can't say I feel for the brother; anybody dumb enough to hurt you deserves whatever he gets in life and in love." I pulled her close to me and rubbed her back.

Her hand reached for me under the sheets, and she began to rub me with the tip of her finger.

"Are you sure you were a virgin? If so, you sure learned quick, huh? You need to quit lying!"

She pushed me on my back and climbed on top of me, laughing.

The sun beaming through my window woke me on Christmas morning. I rolled over, picked up the phone, and dialed Chrys' number. When her voicemail picked up, I hung up the phone. I dialed her cell number, and the voicemail picked up as well. I made one last feeble attempt to reach her on her Blackberry. I typed and sent the message— *Good AM. Merry Xmas!*

After a few moments, I got a reply. *Merry Xmas 2 U!*

? r u?

Out! Cn't tlk rt nw, wl ck bck ltr!

I felt my anger rise as I sat up in bed with visions of Chrys and her husband reconciling and celebrating Christmas morning together.

I prayed, "Lord, I have feelings for this woman that I never felt before. I know I may be wrong for praying about a relationship with a woman that is married, but I need for you to help me. Please let this work, I love her. I don't want to get hurt again, and I need for you to protect my heart. Please don't let her hurt me, and let this work out."

After waiting another fifteen minutes, I concluded that Chrys was not going to call. Frustrated, I walked into my bathroom and started the shower. "Where is she at?" I said out loud.

"Right here!"

I nearly jumped out of my skin, when I looked up and saw Chrys standing in the doorway wearing a trench coat and a Santa hat, laughing.

"Jeez, girl, you could get shot like that!" I kissed her. "How did you get in here?"

"I unlocked the back door while you were in the bathroom last night. I figured you wouldn't check it before you went to bed last night."

"That's why you weren't home this morning?" I asked, relieved.

"I was on my way over here. I wanted to surprise you. That's also why I didn't answer my cell either."

"Girl, I was having flashbacks of Thanksgiving Day for a minute there."

"Well, are you surprised?" She opened her coat to reveal a red corset with a matching garter and stockings, which she knew I had admired in the Victoria's Secret catalog. "I wore special 'Vickies' just for you. Merry Christmas!"

An hour later, as we were getting dressed, my phone rang. "Merry Christmas," I said, too busy admiring Chrys to look at the caller ID.

"Merry Christmas, Koby," Rhea sang. "Are you up?"

"Yeah, why?"

I had talked to Rhea a couple of times since Thanksgiving and our conversations had been brief. True to her word, she kept it on the friend level.

"I was going to swing by this morning so we could exchange gifts."

"Not a good idea. Besides, I didn't get you anything." I glanced over at Chrys. I couldn't understand Rhea thinking we would exchange gifts. She knew I was involved with Chrys, and she made it known she was still seeing Michael.

"Koby, I must say I am disappointed. That's okay. It is the season for giving. I can still drop your gift off."

"Today is not a good day. I will call you later, okay?" I said as Chrys watched me in the mirror.

"Well, be sure to do that, Koby. Tell your family I said Merry Christmas," she said as she hung up the phone.

"I take it Rhea is gonna show up for Christmas dinner?"

"Huh?" I asked. "How did you know it was Rhea?"

"Boy, please . . . you standing there talking on the phone, looking around the room like someone got a spy cam on you. I knew if it wasn't her, it had to be someone. Determined, isn't she?" Chrys looked at me inquisitively.

"*Worrisome* is more like it."

"You must've really turned her out?"

I walked up behind her. "Did I turn you out?"

"I think you got it twisted, boo—I am the one that has you open, Mr. Lickety-split!"

She laughed as I picked her up and threw her on the bed. We began kissing, and soon her hand was under my shirt. "We are gonna be late," she said, as I began sucking on her neck.

"They'll understand. My parents probably are stuck in traffic anyway." I rubbed her nipples.

"Koby, you are about to start something you can't finish." She began to unbutton my jeans.

"Believe me, you started this a long time ago, baby."

The sound of the doorbell startled us, and we sat up quickly.

"Be right back!" I headed down the steps, praying that Rhea hadn't been on her cell phone when she called and decided to come over anyway. I opened the front door cautiously.

"Merry Christmas, Koby!" Momma said as she hugged me.

"Merry Christmas, Momma!" I looked at her with surprise. "What are you doing here, Momma? Where's Pop and Jaamell?"

"They are in the car. We just stopped by on the way to Dorian's." She yelled up the steps, "Merry Christmas, Chrys!" and whispered to me, "I saw her car parked in the driveway."

"Merry Christmas, Mrs. Jackson." Chrys, looking cute as a button in her Santa hat, red windsuit, and white K-Swiss, blushed as she came down the steps.

I smiled when I thought of what was under her clothes.

Momma gave her a big hug and winked at me. "Well, we'd better get going. Are you all ready, or am I interrupting?"

"No, Ma. Chrys just stopped by this morning to give me my gift. It's beautiful. Show it to her, baby."

Chrys' eyes got as big as saucers as I bent over with laughter.

Momma looked at us and smiled.

"I'll show it to her later, sweetie!" Chrys smiled through clenched teeth.

"Later is fine, Chrys," Momma said, "but we need to be going."

"We are right behind you, Ma. I just need to load the gifts into my car."

"Well, come on then. We'll wait," Momma said knowingly.

I looked at Chrys, who by this time had begun to put on her trench coat. We took the armloads of gifts and put them into the trunk and on the back seat of my car. Then we all headed to Dorian's.

The traditional Christmas brunch was terrific, as usual. The house was filled with the sound of traditional Motown Christmas carols. The girls ran through the house playing with their countless toys.

After we all ate, Dorian announced it was time for the adults to exchange gifts. We all went into the living room, and Jackie began to play Santa's helper by passing out the gifts, which we had placed under the tree when we first arrived.

"Oh, baby, thank you!" Momma said as she removed the porcelain angel music box from the wrapping. She twisted the key and the tune "O, How I Love Jesus" began to play. It was one of her favorite hymns.

Dad was just as pleased with the gift Dorian and I had gotten him and Uncle Theodore—a weekend at Myrtle Beach to play golf!

Chrys had gotten Momma a beautiful leather journal with her initials engraved on the front, but the funniest recipient was Jaamell—he received a pair of Jordans from me, Dorian, Jackie, Chela, *and* Chrys!

"I got a pair for every day of the week!" he yelled as he opened the box from Chrys.

"That is a shame," Momma said. "All of you are crazy for spending that kind of money on a pair of tennis shoes."

When Momma wasn't looking, Dad whispered in my ear, "I forgot the pair I got him in the back of my truck."

When it was time for Chrys to open her gifts, she reached in her purse and removed a small, gold-wrapped box. "Merry Christmas." She handed it to me.

"I thought you said she gave you your gift earlier?" Momma asked.

"Uh . . . she . . . we—"

Jackie cackled and tossed her head back. "I bet she did!"

"Shut up, Jackie!" I kissed Chrys, who looked as if she wanted to go through the floor. "Thank you, baby."

Chrys nodded towards the box. "You open yours first."

I reached and gave her the small box I had for her. "Let's open it together," I told her.

We sat on the sofa and opened the boxes simultaneously. She screamed when she opened hers, and I shook my head in amazement when I saw mine.

"What?" Jackie ran over to see for herself. She screeched when she saw the gifts. "They got each other the same thing!"

"I thought you were looking at these for yourself," I said. I reached into the box and removed the earrings we were both admiring in the jewelry showcase at the mall. We both removed the earrings we already wore and put our new ones in. I reached in my jacket and removed the other box I had been holding.

Chrys smiled. "Another gift?"

"You gave me two." I kissed the tip of her nose.

She opened the box and removed the matching pendant.

She passed it to me, and I reached around and helped her put it on her neck. "Beautiful," I told her.

"I know. I love it." She smiled and looked at me affectionately.

"I wasn't talking about the necklace."

"Oh."

"I was talking about you—you are beautiful. I love you."

"Koby, I love you too!" She cried and hugged me.

We heard everyone sing behind us, "Awwwwww!".

Chapter 15

"Where Will You Go"

—Babyface

Brenda poked her head into my office. "Koby, our flight leaves at eight in the morning; we need to be at the airport by seven."

"I'll be there," I told her, looking up from my desk.

"That's not my concern—I need for you to be there *on time*. I don't want you to be looking like O.J.," she said jokingly, "flying through the airport, trying not to miss your flight."

"You just worry about your big presentation; that should be your only concern—it's called *job security*."

"Well, you miss that flight tomorrow and you won't have a job to be secure about, Mr. Smart Alec," she said as she left out.

I sat back down and began finishing the reports I had to present this week at the finance conference in Boston. I looked up at the clock and the numbers. It was well after eight o'clock. I hadn't realized it was that late.

I stood up to stretch. I felt my phone vibrating on my hip and flipped it open to read the message—*Still working?*

I replied back to Chrys' pager, *Yep, leaving now.*

She sent back—*I miss U, cll whn u gt to the car.*

I gathered all of my papers and files, placing them into my briefcase. I grabbed my coat and the hat and gloves Chrys got me as a stocking gift and headed out the door. I noticed light coming from Tim's office and knocked on the door.

"Open," he called out.

"You still working?"

"Yeah, I'll be finished in a minute."

"See you in the morning then."

"Yeah. Bren already came in and gave me the 'be-tardy-and-die' speech."

"Me too." I laughed. "I'm surprised she's not picking us up in the morning."

"I bet that thought did run across her mind though."

"Well, see you in the morning," I told him as I left his office.

I walked across the empty parking lot to my car. I pulled my hat over my ears, grateful for it, because the cold drizzle combined with the January temperature did not feel all that great. I unlocked the doors and got in, started the engine, and blasted the heat in an attempt to get warm. I took my gloves off and picked up my cell phone. I dialed Chrys' number.

"Hey, baby," she answered.

"Hey, watchadoin'?" I rubbed my hands to-gether to generate some heat.

"Watching *American Idol.* You cold?"

"Yeah. You trying to warm a brother up?"

"Of course. Are you coming to me, or do you want me to come to you?"

"I was thinking we'd cum together." I laughed slyly. "I gotta go home and pack, and then I'll come over there."

"Okay. Are you hungry?" She giggled.

"Always for you, baby."

"I meant for food, jerk."

"No, I can grab some McDonald's on the way home. You just be ready with my dessert when I get there."

She sighed. "I think I can manage that."

Later that night as we lay in bed, I thought about how much my life had changed since I'd met Chrys. It was as if my life had come full circle. Since Christmas Day, it felt like every waking mo-ment I thought of nothing else but her.

"When are you flying back?" she asked.

"Friday evening. Are you gonna pick me up from the airport?"

"You know I am. I'm going to the kitchen to get some juice. You want something?"

"What I want is right here in this bed." I rolled over on top of her.

"Move, silly." She laughed and pushed me out of the bed, and ran down the steps before I had a chance to recover.

The phone rang and then quickly stopped. I

knew she'd answered it. I looked over at the clock on her nightstand. "One eighteen," the numbers shouted at me.

"Kind of late for a phone call, isn't it?" I said as she got back into bed.

"Yeah." She got under the covers.

"Who was it?"

She turned over and looked at me.

I instantly knew who it was. "It was him, wasn't it?" I glared at her. I felt the heat began to rise to my head when she didn't answer me. "It was him, wasn't it?"

She looked down. "Koby—"

"What the hell is he calling for at one in the morning?"

"I don't know."

I sat on the side of the bed. "What do you mean, you don't know?"

"I don't know," she said a little louder. "What is your deal? I didn't even talk to him."

"My 'deal' is your ex calling you at one in the morning and you acting like it's all good." I stood and began getting dressed.

"Okay, hold up. I think we need to calm down before this really gets out of control." She stood up.

"I think I need to leave so you can have time to *talk* to your husband. I'm out." I walked down the steps.

She came running behind me. "Koby, don't be like this!" She grabbed my arm.

"No, Chrys. I thought I could handle this because you told me it was over between you two, but obviously it's not."

"What do you mean?" She stared angrily at me.

"I'm saying I'll talk to you later." I walked out the door, leaving her stunned.

"Hello," Dorian groaned into the phone.

"*D*, you up?" I tried not to sound like it wasn't seven-thirty in the morning.

"Man, no, I'm not up. What?"

"I need a favor."

"What is it, Koby? Come on, man, I'm sleepy, and Jackie is gonna be coming in here in a minute talking about get up."

"I need you to pick my car up from the airport. My flight is about to board in a minute."

"That's right, you going to Boston this morning. Where is Chrys? Why didn't she take you to the airport?"

"Long story. Can you please just get my car? And I'm gonna need you to pick me up Friday afternoon too."

"No problem. But what happened between you and Chrys?"

The ticket agent began to call for boarding.

"I gotta go, *D*. I'll call you later." I turned my phone off and reluctantly went to board the plane. I double-checked my phone before turning it off.

I tried to sleep on the flight with no success. I couldn't believe what had happened the night before. One minute I was in total bliss with Chrys in my arms, the next I was riding home by myself, pumping Tupac's "Me Against the World." I tried to tell myself that this was for the best, that I had found out about Chrys' continual relationship with her husband *before* I got in any deeper.

The first day of the conference was filled with the usual introductions and hobnobbing with other company managers. There were formal training sessions as well as open-discussion forums. Secretly wishing the day would end, I went through the motions, pretending to be interested.

"Koby, you want to meet us in the lobby for dinner around seven?" Brenda asked.

"Naw, I'm tired. I'm just gonna go to my room and get some sleep."

"You sure?" she asked, looking worried.

"Are you all right, Koby? You've been quiet all day, man."

"I'm okay. You guys go ahead and have a good time at the company's expense." I tried to smile.

I went up to my room and took off my jacket and tie. I picked up my cell phone and dialed my home number. I let it ring until I heard the sound of my own voice. I pressed my access code and checked my messages.

I had three new messages: *Hey, Koby, I just wanted to let you know I was thinking about you because today is your big trip, and let you know how much I love you. Remember, you're blessed and highly favored and God's got your back because you're special.*

I love you too, Ma.

Second message: *Koby, man, I hope you know I owe you a knock upside the head for waking me up this morning. I got your car. I told Jaamell he could use it for the rest of the week while you're away—just kidding! But, yo, call me and tell me what happened. Peace.*

"Thanks, *D*. Always there when I need you, but you are not the voice I'm hoping to hear right now," I said to no one.

I listened for the last message. There was a long silence and I could hear breathing on the line. I strained my ear, hoping to hear her say something. Just as I was about to hang up and call her back, I heard something else: *Hi, Koby, sorry about that. It's me. I just wanted to remind you that my birthday is in two weeks, and I'd really like for us to go out. I'll call you soon to confirm.*

Rhea . . . What is with this girl? I know I hadn't been giving her any signals that I was interested. If anything, I was acting disinterested, but she just wouldn't let it go.

I waited on the line long enough to find out that there were no more messages. I lay across the bed, staring at the TV, not watching, but thinking. She didn't even try to call me last night after I left. *You did the right thing, Koby,* I told myself. *It was time to leave it alone. You don't need the drama anyway.* I convinced myself that I didn't have time to wait in limbo for a woman who couldn't decide whether or not she still wanted to be with her cheating, abusive husband. If she could not see what I was worth, then it was her loss.

I picked up the phone and called Dorian. "Hey, *D*," I greeted him solemnly.

"What's up, Koby? You a'ight, man?"

"Yeah, I'm cool."

"Your presentation go all right?"

"It's not until tomorrow."

"Okay, man, now what happened?"

"*D*, why is that nigga calling her at one o'clock in the morning? And she's answering the phone and chitchatting with him like everything's hunky-dory. Then when I ask her, 'What he wanted?', she says, "It's nothing.'" I felt the anger from the night before return.

"So what did you say to her?"

"I told her fine, she can go be with him, if that's what she wanna do. I don't have time to be no-body's second choice, *D*; I just went through this crap with Rhea, you know that."

"You're wrong, Koby."

"What? What do you mean, I'm wrong? Come on, *D*, I was the dumb one, trying to be the good, caring boyfriend, when the entire time she was screwing Michael. In the end, *I* was the one that got screwed!"

"Koby, first of all, calm the hell down. Now, I know Rhea did some foul stuff, but we aren't talk-ing about Rhea. Speaking of which . . . didn't she just call you around midnight one day last week? As much as you hate talking to her and as much as you brush her off, can you stop her from calling you?"

"No."

"Exactly! And when she calls, are you not at least civil to her?"

"Yeah."

"Koby, you can't even stop Rhea from popping up at the crib. You know why?—because you can't control what she does. Now keeping all of that in mind, how can Chrys stop her husband from call-ing her?"

I sat silent, listening to Dorian call me out and wake me up to the situation.

"Koby, I need for you to realize that every woman is not out to get you. You can not let that one relationship mess with your head or your heart."

"You're right, *D*," I mumbled.

"You also have to realize that the girl was married—still married, technically. And that means she has some baggage. You got some too. What you gotta figure out is if you love her enough to deal with all that. You have to trust her and have faith in your relationship that she loves you enough not to do anything to hurt you. It's gonna be hard as hell, but if you really love her, you can make it happen."

"True words from a man married to a woman with two baby daddies." I laughed.

"Believe me, it ain't easy, but I love Jackie enough to deal with any crap them baby daddies dish out."

"A'ight, *D*. You're right."

"You really love this girl, Koby?"

"Yeah, *D*, I believe I do."

"Then handle your business, son."

I hung up and picked up my phone. I typed the words "I am sorry!" and hit the *send* button. I waited, watching for a response. I closed my eyes and whispered the words, "Please, Lord."

A few moments later, the phone began to dance across the nightstand. *Call me*, the words said across the screen.

"Thank you, God," I said aloud. I picked up the phone and dialed Chrys' number.

After two rings, I heard her voice on the other end. "Hello."

"Hi," I said. "How are you?"

"Fine. I'm good."

"Oh."

There was an awkward silence between us, and I didn't know what to say.

"How is the conference?"

"Good. A lot of good info," I responded.

"Look, this is too formal for me, okay. So how about I say what I have to say and you say what you have to say and we move on?"

"Okay, go ahead."

"All right. First of all, believe it or not, this is not easy for either one of us. We both are just coming out of committed relationships and are very vulnerable right now. We both have these trust issues, but you have to trust me enough to know that if I say, 'It's over between me and him,' then it is. The same way I have to trust that it's over between you and Rhea, even though she is still an uninvited guest at your family functions. If you say you no longer have feelings for her, then I have to take your word for it; you owe me that same respect."

"You're right, and I apologize. Am I forgiven?"

"That's it?"

"Am I forgiven?"

"I'll think about it."

I could hear her smiling through the phone. I felt an air of relief between the both of us.

"Please? I'll make it up to you, I promise."

"Yeah, yeah, yeah."

I heard her fumbling in the background. "What are you doing?" I asked.

"Lying in bed, eating ice-cream."

I laughed. "You're such a tease."

We talked until we fell asleep.

The next day as we were making our depart-ment presentation, I felt my phone vibrating on my hip. I quickly answered the questions directed at me and made my way back to my seat. I flipped my pager open and read the message from Chrys: *Call me at home*, ASAP.

I checked the time and realized that it was only ten o'clock in the morning. I wondered if she was sick, because she obviously wasn't at work.

"I gotta go make a phone call," I whispered to Tim, who was sitting beside me. When I got up from my seat, Brenda looked at me like I had lost my mind. "I'll be right back."

I went into the lobby of the hotel and called Chrys from my cell phone. "Hey, baby, what's wrong?"

"I gotta go home," she said barely above a whis-per.

"Aren't you at home?"

"No, Koby. Home, home—to Georgia."

"What happened?"

"My mother is sick, and I have to go be with her. I am leaving in a little while. I got a twelve-thirty flight."

"Oh, baby, I am so sorry. You need me to come?"

"No, I'll be okay. I'll probably be there for a cou-ple of days."

"Okay, do you need anything?"

"No, I'm gonna catch a cab to the airport. I don't know exactly when I'm coming back."

I heard her sniffling and wanted more than anything at that moment to be there for her. "Chrys, baby, don't cry. It's gonna be all right, I promise. Get yourself together, okay. Call me as soon as you get there and let me know what's going on." Just then I saw Brenda peeping out the door. "I gotta get back to this meeting. I'll page you later. I love you."

"I love you too, Koby."

I went back to into the conference praying she'd be okay.

Chapter 16

"Before I Let You Go"

—BLACKstreet

At around four, Chrys paged me to let me know that she had made it and was on her way to the hospital. I responded saying that I loved her and she should call me when she got settled.

I decided to join Tim and Brenda for dinner in order to get out of the hotel and occupy my mind. We went to Legal Seafood and enjoyed their delicious clam chowder.

After dinner we headed back to the hotel, barely able to keep our eyes open because we were so full.

"You guys did an awesome job today," Brenda told us as we were on the elevator.

"Hey, you didn't do so bad yourself, Bren." I nudged Tim.

"He's right, Brenda; you made us proud." Tim smiled.

The elevator stopped on our floor, and we all got out.

"Job security!" Brenda yelled as she entered her room.

We all laughed.

I had just gotten into the shower, when I heard my cell phone ringing. I grabbed a towel and ran to answer it, almost breaking my neck in the process. "Hello," I panted into the phone.

"Hey, are you busy? You are all out of breath. I can call you back later."

The sound of Chrys' voice caused me to smile. "No, I'm good. I was in the shower. How is everything going? Your mom okay?"

"She's resting right now. I just checked into the hotel to take a shower and change. It's been a long day."

"Why are you staying in a hotel?"

"It's easier to get to the hospital from the hotel in case something happens. Traffic in ATL can be horrific, and I just didn't feel like dealing with it. It's just for a few days; then I'll stay at the house. Besides, my Visa can only hold so much." She sighed.

"What happened to your mom, Chrys?"

"They found a mass in her breast."

"Oh, I'm sorry. What are the doctors saying?"

"They are performing surgery tomorrow morning, and then she'll begin a round of chemotherapy. I'll probably be here for a couple of weeks."

"Chrys, you are handling this all by yourself? What about the rest of your family?"

"My aunts are older, and my cousins have their own lives to deal with. I'll be okay."

"Baby, do you need me to do anything?"

"Pray—I know you can do that. And just knowing that you're there for me is comfort enough. Thank you."

I could hear her crying softly into the phone. "Baby, please don't cry." I felt tears forming in my eyes. "You are telling me to pray, but you gotta have faith and know that your mother is gonna be healed; prayers are worthless without faith."

"You're right," she said. "I always feel better when I talk to you."

"Good. That's another one of those qualities my grandmother passed on to me."

She giggled. "All right, Mr. Jackson, go and finish your shower. I will call you back tomorrow."

"You go and get yourself together. Text me in the morning, if you need me."

"Okay. I love you, Koby."

"I love you too." I hit the *end* button on the phone and sat on the side of the bed for what seemed like hours.

I decided to call Momma and let her know what was going on.

"That's terrible," she said after I explained Chrys' situation. "Does she need for us to do anything?"

"She just said to pray."

"Well, we can definitely do that. You really love her, don't you, Koby?"

"Momma, I do—I can't explain it; I want to make it my priority to make her happy."

"Spoken like a man in love. You keep that priority and you can't go wrong—take it from a woman."

"Thanks, Mom. Where is Pop and Jaamell?"

"Your father is in the garage, and Jaamell is in

his room. Koby, he said something about staying with you for the summer and getting some kind of internship. Do you know what he is talking about?"

"Rhea mentioned something about getting him one at the firm. I don't know any more than that."

"Well, be careful . . . and I am gonna leave it at that."

"Okay, I will. I gotta go, Mom. Tell *J* to call me. Love you.

"Love you too. See you Sunday."

The remainder of the conference went well. Brenda, Tim, and I really made a good impression with the department heads and other managers. We were on cloud nine by the time we were on the plane headed home.

Dorian was at the airport when I got there.

"I'm surprised you're on time," I told him as we walked to the baggage claim area.

"You'd better be glad I came and got you at all," he told me.

I introduced him to Brenda and Tim as we waited for our luggage to come around the turnstile.

"Why didn't you tell me you knew him?" Brenda quipped.

I shrugged. "The subject never came up."

Dorian signed autographs for their kids and promised Brenda he'd consider speaking at the company scholarship banquet. We grabbed our bags and headed for the parking lot.

As we got in his Jag, Dorian asked, "How's Chrys' mom?"

"She's pretty sick, but that was to be expected. The doctors have given her a good prognosis, though."

"That's good. Jackie talked to her the other night. I feel bad that she is there by herself."

"I know. I want to go and be with her."

"Then go. It's Friday. What else do you have planned for the weekend?—your woman ain't here."

"I know, but—"

"Get out."

I looked at him like he was crazy. "What?"

"Get out and come on." He got out of the car and took my bags out of the trunk.

"Dorian, quit playing, man," I said as I got out and followed him back into the airport.

Dorian walked up to the ticket counter and asked the agent, "When is the next flight to Atlanta?"

"In about two hours," the man said without looking up.

"Does another airline have one sooner?"

"Don't know. You have to check with them."

"What?" Dorian said, pissed by his nonchalance. This caused the man to look up. "Oh my! You're Dorian Silver. I'm sorry, Mr. Silver. I believe there is a flight leaving in about thirty minutes on USAir. Can I have your autograph, sir?"

"You'll have to check with me later." Dorian headed toward the other counter.

I rushed behind him. "Dorian, what are you doing?"

"Can I get a ticket on the next flight to Atlanta?" he asked the woman.

"Coach is booked up, sir. We do have some first-class seats available. I can get you one if you like, but it's boarding right now."

Dorian whipped out his credit card and told me to give the lady my ID.

Security quickly went through my luggage.

Dorian looked at me as I turned to leave. I gave him a hug. "*D*, man, thanks."

"Hurry up. I'm paying for parking."

I rushed to the boarding gate and got to my seat. I sat back and relaxed, happy with thoughts of seeing Chrys.

The two-hour plane ride went by quickly. *I gotta fly first-class more often.*

As I stood at the baggage claim for the second time that evening, I dialed Chrys' cell number.

"Hey, you made it home?" she asked.

"Yeah." I tried not to smile. "Where are you?"

"Still at the hospital. They're about to give Mama a sedative to help her sleep. As soon as she is settled, I'll be leaving. How was your trip? Was Dorian on time to meet you?"

"Yeah, Dorian always comes through for me. What hotel did you say you were staying in?"

"Atlanta Hilton on Courtland."

"The one near the airport?"

"Yep, that's the one."

I heard the nurse come in and begin to talk to her.

"Hey, go ahead and make sure your mom is okay. I'll talk to you later."

"Okay. I'll call you when I get to the room."

"All right, baby. I love you."

"Love you too."

I hung the phone and headed to the florist located inside the airport. I purchased a dozen roses and caught the shuttle to the airport. I waited for about thirty minutes in the hotel bar and then paged Chrys—*Where r u?*

She sent back—*Jst gttng 2 the hotel. Call me in 5 min*

? rm r u n?

1542 Y?

Call u n a minute

I went to the restaurant and ordered two steak and shrimp dinners and a bottle of wine to be delivered to the room in thirty minutes. I had just walked back into the hotel lobby, when Chrys walked in. I ducked back into the restaurant before she could see me.

She went to the front desk for a minute then got on the elevator.

I gave her enough time to get to her room and then called her cell number.

She answered, "Hi, baby."

"Hi, yourself. What are you doing?" I asked as I rode the elevator to her floor.

"About to get in the shower."

"Um . . . sounds good to me. You want me to join you?"

"Sure, I'd like that," she said playfully. "You want me to wait until you catch the plane?"

"Naw, you go ahead. I'll be there in time to wash

your back. Did you eat yet?" I was now standing outside of her door, grinning from ear to ear.

"No, I'll probably get some Mickey D's later."

I tapped on the door lightly.

"Hold on. Sounds like someone is at the door."

I could hear her voice coming towards me.

"Who is it?"

"Room service, ma'am."

"I didn't order room service." She unlocked the door.

"Surprise!"

She stood with her mouth open. "Koby, oh baby!" She hugged me so tight, I had no doubt she was glad to see me.

Noticing she was still fully dressed, I said, "Hey, I thought you were getting in the shower."

"I was. Don't you hear the water running." She led me to see the bathroom fogged with steam.

I gave her the roses. "These are for you."

"Thanks. They are so beautiful." She placed them on the nightstand.

"Like you."

I could see she was tired. Her eyes had bags under them, and she looked fatigued.

We sat down on the side of the bed, and I began to rub her back.

"How did—where—I don't care; I am just glad you're here."

"I wanted to be here, baby." I pulled her to me and held her in my arms as she began to cry. "Shh, baby. It's okay. Go ahead; I'm here now. I know it's been a rough week."

Chrys finally straightened up and looked at me. "I must look crazy." She smiled weakly.

"Tired is a good look for you; I like it." I hugged her close.

There was a knock at the door. She looked confused. "Who is that?" She walked over to the door. "Who is it?"

"Room service," the voice announced from the other side of the door.

This time she looked out the peephole. She opened the door and turned to me as the bellboy wheeled in the cart of food. She shook her head in disbelief. "You never cease to amaze me, JaKoby Jackson."

"It's not the Mickey D's you wanted, but it is edible. Go ahead and jump in the shower. The food will still be warm when you get out."

She kissed me as she went into the bathroom.

I tipped the bellboy.

"Will there be anything else, sir?"

"Do you know where I can get some candles?"

"I can get you some from the kitchen, but they're not scented or anything."

"That's okay. I'll take 'em; matter of fact, I'll come down and get them myself."

He smiled at me. "That'd probably be quicker."

"Chrys, I'll be right back," I yelled into the bathroom.

"Where you going?"

"Downstairs right quick, come on." I grabbed the key card from the nightstand, and we quickly rushed to get the candles.

It must've really been quick, because Chrys was still in the bathroom when I got back upstairs. I set the candles in the middle of the small dining table and found a jazz station on the clock radio. I dimmed the lights and stood back to look at the ambiance I'd created in a matter of minutes. "Not bad," I said, thinking out loud.

The bathroom door opened, and she came out looking refreshed. "This is so nice. I feel so underdressed." She looked down at her ensemble.

"You look perfect." I took her by the hand and led her to the table. I noticed the State University T-shirt she had on. "Isn't that mine?"

"Guilty—I wanted to feel close to you."

"Awww, that is so special. Give me a kiss." I reached for her.

She backed away laughing. "Move, a sister is hungry. I haven't had a decent meal all week. We can play later."

"Promises, promises."

I sat down across from her, and we ate and enjoyed each other's company, which we'd missed all week.

"I am so full-*itis* is setting in." She sat back in her chair. "What?—no dessert, Mr. Perfect?"

"I have cake, Ms. Thang." I walked and stood behind her.

"Oh, really?" She looked up at me and smiled. "Go ahead and take your shower; I'll clear all of this up."

I got my shaving kit and my shorts out of my suitcase and headed into the bathroom. By the time I came out of the bathroom, Chrys had fallen asleep at the head of the bed.

I lifted her and placed her under the comforter and got in bed next to her.

She rolled over and placed her head on my chest. "Koby?"

"Yeah, boo."

"I love you so much."

"I love you too." I kissed the top of her head and went to sleep.

Chapter 17
"...Where I Wanna Be"
—Donnell Jones

The weekend with Chrys flew by. Before I knew it, it was late Sunday evening and we were waiting for me to board my flight. "I'm gonna miss you, sweetheart." I rubbed my hand across her cheek.

She looked at me with those beautiful eyes. "I'm sorry we really didn't get to hang out this weekend."

"This wasn't a pleasure trip, remember?"

"I know. Thank you so much for coming."

"Maybe next time I can meet your mother."

"Definitely. It will be under better circumstances."

The announcer called for first-class boarding.

"Wow! *First-class*—I'm impressed."

"Compliments of Dorian Silver." I kissed her fully on the mouth. "I will call you when I get home, baby."

"Okay."

I could tell she was about to cry, so I gave her a quick hug and turned away.

"I love you, Koby."

"I love you too, Chrys." I waved and gave the agent my boarding pass.

As I sat back and prepared for takeoff, I thought about all the advice that I had gotten from my parents and Dorian over the years when it came to love. I knew that I wanted to spend the rest of my life with Chrys Matthews; I had no doubt she was the love of my life. I just prayed that she felt the same way.

I drifted off to sleep with Chrys in my heart but woke up with Rhea on my mind. I don't know what made her creep into my dream, but she was the first thought that I had when the stewardess woke me to tell me to fasten my seat belt. Momma's words rang out to me: "Be careful."

I was folding clothes Thursday night. Chrys had been in Atlanta for two weeks, and I was really thinking about flying back to see her.

Rhea whined through the phone, "Koby, my birthday is tomorrow night. Please . . . at least have a drink with me. Come on . . ."

"Rhea, no. I don't think that's a good idea."

"Koby, I don't want to spend my birthday alone."

"What about Charisse and Jeff?"

"Koby, I don't want to be 'the third wheel.' "

I stood up and began to put the clothes away. "What about Michael?"

"*Funny*, Koby—you know he and I aren't like that."

"I don't know how you and he are, Rhea."

"Look, you said we would always be friends. Can we please at least meet for drinks tomorrow night? I can give you the application for Jaamell's summer job in the mailroom. It has to be turned in by February 15 in order to be considered."

Today is the fifth, and Jaamell had been worrying me to death about getting it. "Fine, Rhea, but it's gonna be early—I mean that. I'll meet you at Jernigan's at six. Drinks—that's it—and I'm doing this for Jaamell."

"God! Koby, you don't have to act like it's community service, for Christ sake; I just want us to hang out like old times."

"Okay, we'll do that. Now I gotta go. I'll see you tomorrow."

"Bye, Koby."

I hung the phone up convincing myself that I was doing this for Jaamell. *Rhea and I are just friends and that's okay. Besides, it's her birthday. Chrys is still friends with her ex; I can be friends with Rhea.*

I was still telling myself that as I pulled into the parking lot of Jernigan's Sports Bar. I saw Rhea's car two spaces over from mine. I took a couple of deep breaths as I opened the door. I walked to the coat check and got a ticket.

"Koby!" I heard her call my name from a corner table.

Damn, she looks good. She let her hair grow out a bit and had it neatly flipped in a bob. Her body was still the epitome of perfection, and she looked elegant in her black cashmere sweater and slacks.

"Hey, Rhea. Happy birthday." I gave her a quick peck on the cheek and handed her the card and small bouquet of flowers I'd picked up on the way.

She smiled. "Oh, you didn't have to do this."

"It is your birthday."

We ordered a round of drinks and caught up on each other's lives. Before I knew it, it was eight o'clock.

"Wow, it's late!" she said. "You wanna grab something to eat?"

"No, I think I'm gonna pass. Besides, I'm sure you already have plans to party the rest of the night away."

"No. I think I might treat myself to a movie though."

"You? A movie? I never thought I'd hear that from your mouth."

"Whatever, Koby. Thank you so much. You made my birthday. Oh, here's the application for Jaamell. I'll get it from you before the deadline." She reached into her bag and gave me the manila envelope.

"Thanks, Rhea. I appreciate you looking out for him."

"Hey, he's practically family." She stood to leave. "Walk me to my car?"

"Yeah, let me grab my coat." I turned my ticket in and got my things.

"Cute hat," she commented as we walked to her car.

"Thanks. Well, I guess this is goodbye." I opened her door for her. "I really had a nice time, Rhea."

"Me too. Talk to you later." She hugged me and got into her car. She rolled her window down and said, "I like being your friend, Koby. Thanks for everything," and she pulled off.

I walked to my car and put the envelope in my

trunk. I checked my cell phone and saw that I had missed three calls. I realized that I didn't take my phone off silent mode when I left work and that Chrys had called me twice. *Don't panic*, I thought. *Just tell her you went out. Leave it at that. It's not lying, and what she doesn't know won't hurt her. Besides, she has more to deal with on her plate than what you're doing while she's not here.*

I decided to call Dorian first, since he was the last person that called. "What's up, *D*?"

"Hey, Koby. Where you at, man?"

"I'm just leaving Jernigan's. I decided to come by here for happy hour after I got off today."

"By yourself?" he asked, surprised. "How was it?"

"It was cool. What are you doing tonight?"

"Chilling, I guess. It's too cold to go out."

"You mean you don't wanna floss in the fur?"

"Naw. I'll strut my stuff for Jackie later." He laughed. "You coming through for the fight?"

"Of course. I wanna see Lennox whup Holyfield's old behind."

"We'll see . . . and I'm gonna leave it at that."

"A'ight, see you later, *D*."

"Peace."

I waited until I got home to call Chrys. I wanted time to get myself together and decide what to tell her.

"Hey, sweetie."

"Hey, Koby. I called you, but you didn't answer earlier."

"I know. My cell was on silent. I forgot to turn the ringer on after work. How are you doing?"

"Okay. Hopefully Mama will be released Monday—that's my good news for the day."

"Baby, that's great—that means you can come home soon."

"Yeah. I'll still be here for a little while though, but at least I don't have to be in this hotel room. My credit cards can't take much more. I'll be staying at the house with her."

"How long do you think you'll be down there?" I asked, disappointed.

"Just a little while longer. I know I'll miss your birthday, but I promise you I'll make it up to you."

"It's not my birthday that I'm talking about, Chrys—I want to be with you every day."

"Koby, you are so sweet. I'll be back home soon. You'd better be good, though. You know I was suspicious when you didn't answer your phone. I thought the diva had gotten her claws back into you."

"You are crazy." I laughed nervously. "The only woman that has her claws in me is you. I love you."

"Love you too, Koby."

I hung the phone up feeling like the jerk I was.

After dinner on Sunday, I gave Jaamell the application. He was all excited about having a real summer job. Momma, on the other hand, was not enthused.

"Ma, this is a real opportunity for him," I told her as we sat in the den.

"Come on, Ma," Jaamell pleaded, "I really want to do this."

"Why can't you get a job around here, Jaamell? There are plenty of summer jobs available."

"Not in a top law firm," I responded.

"I don't know, Koby . . . I think there is something else to this." Momma glared at me.

"Momma, I know what you are thinking. Believe me, I have this under control. Rhea knows that we are just friends. I am just looking at this as something good for Jaamell."

"And I appreciate it, bro. And if you happen to get 'some' in the process—"

Momma hollered, "Jaamell JaKoby Jackson, boy, I will knock your behind out! Get your disrespectful butt to your room and study!"

"The harder I try, the harder you make it for me, *J*." I shook my head as he left the room. "I'm sorry, Ma."

She looked at me. "And you think you want to deal with that all summer?"

"I can handle him. You know I can. It'll be good or him, and this will give you and Pop a chance to do some things this summer . . . like travel."

"JaKoby, you know your father is not going anywhere without Theodore." She laughed.

"He might, especially if you mention golf."

"I'll think about it. But, Koby, I need for you to think about it too. Women have a way of doing things. I don't want you to find yourself in a situation you never wanted to be in, in the first place. You'd better look at this real good."

"I will, Ma, I promise." I gave her a kiss as I rose to leave.

* * *

Later that night, Rhea called, and I told her that I gave Jaamell the application.

"Okay, just make sure you get it to me by the fifteenth. Don't forget, Koby."

"I won't, Rhea."

We talked a little while longer.

Rhea had me laughing as she told me about the remainder of her birthday weekend. "Seriously. The woman was sitting in the theatre, next to her husband, and she translated the entire movie! I was so mad. But get this—she even mocked the moans when they were having sex, as if he couldn't translate that by himself."

"I thought sex was a universal act."

She laughed. "Obviously not!"

I heard a beep in my ear. "Hold on," I said and switched to the other call. "Hello." I laughed into the phone.

"Tell me the joke so I can laugh," Chrys said, catching me off guard.

I tried to sound calm. "Hey, I wasn't expecting your call until later."

"My aunt is here visiting with my mom, so I got a few free minutes. How was church?"

"Good. Hold on a minute"—I clicked back over to Rhea—"Let me call you back, okay?"

"Whatever. I know you aren't, but it's all good. We'll talk later this week. Take care."

I returned to Chrys. "So how's everything going?"

"Okay. Things are getting kind of settled."

"Don't get *too* settled; you gotta come home to your man."

"I know. I miss you."

"I miss you too. When do you think you'll be home?"

"Soon."

We talked for about an hour. She filled me in on her mother's prognosis, and I told her what was going on at work.

"What are you eating?"

"Ice," she replied.

"Interesting."

"What?"

"What can you do with ice?" I asked quietly. "Ever had a hot and cold treatment?"

"Like for a sprained ankle?"

"Something like that. See, I'd give you a hot and cold treatment before I eat cake. I blow air gently on the cake and warm it up real good, then put the ice in my mouth before I eat it."

"Wow! That is interesting! You've gotta give me a treatment next time we have cake and ice-cream."

I could hear her smiling through the phone. "Do you think we might be able to indulge for my birthday?" I asked.

"I'm trying. Hopefully, I'll be able to at least come for the weekend." She sighed.

"Does that mean you'll be my valentine?"

"Any time you want me to," she answered seductively. "Hold up a minute."

I could hear a woman talking in the background and quickly hit the power button on the stereo.

"Hey," she said when she came back to the phone.

"Time's up, huh?"

"Yeah, time's up. I love you. Talk to you tomorrow."

* * *

It was Thursday night when she finally confirmed that she wouldn't be home for my birthday.

"I thought I would be able to get one of my aunts to stay here with Mama," Chrys said, "but no one has given me a definite answer. I am so sorry, baby."

"It's okay. We have so many other birthdays to share. You are where you need to be right now. Your mother is your number one priority. I do come a close second, though."

"That, you do; I will make it up to you when I come home."

I tried not to sound disappointed. "Promise?"

"Promise. I'll even give you a hot and cold treatment," she told me.

"Well, where do you want me to send your Valentine's Day gift?"

"Tell you what—keep it until I get there; it'll give me something to look forward to."

"You don't even want roses?"

"Have them waiting when you pick me up from the airport."

"And when will that be?"

"Sooner than later."

I could hear the doorbell ring.

"Hold on please."

I strained to hear who would be visiting her mom at this time of the night and heard a male voice.

"Well, look who the cat drug in!" she exclaimed.

"Hey, how's my mother-in-law?"

"She's doing better. When did you get here?"

"I came straight from the airport. Can I go back and see her?"

"Hold on, I'm on the phone."

"You're looking good, girl—life must be treating you right."

"Well, *you* sure didn't." Then to me she said, "Hey, my mother has a visitor. I will call you back, okay?"

"Chrys," I said sternly.

"Yeah?"

I inhaled deeply. "Who is that?"

She didn't say anything at first and then said, "I thought we already talked about *trust*, Koby—don't go there."

"Fine. I won't." I hung up the phone before she could say anything else.

I felt my blood begin to boil as I thought about the conversation I overheard. I could not believe that he was there with her, at her mother's house. I began to pace around my living room.

The sound of the doorbell kept me from becoming livid. I peeped through the hole. For some reason, I was glad to see Rhea standing outside.

"Hi, Koby."

I frowned. "Hey, what are you doing here?"

"I told you I'd come by after I left the gym to pick up the application. I have to turn it in tomorrow." She looked at me strangely. "We had this conversation Tuesday, remember?"

"Oh yeah. I forgot."

"I know your birthday is Saturday, but you're not old enough to be senile, are you?"

"Come on in, silly."

She followed me into the living room and sat on

the edge of the sofa. Her hair was pulled back by a headband and I could tell she had on a bodysuit under her bright yellow parka.

"Take off your coat," I said suspiciously.

"No, I'm fine. I won't stay long." She blinked innocently.

"Would you like something to drink?"

"Why are you being so nice to me, Koby?—What do you want?"

"Nothing, Rhea; I'm trying to be hospitable."

"You haven't been this hospitable in a while. I don't know what to think."

"Whatever. I'll be right back."

I went upstairs and grabbed the envelope off my dresser and took a moment to think. *Chrys is chilling with her ex, probably posing as the happy couple for her mom. Rhea and I have really been chilling since her birthday. Maybe I should re-evaluate this entire situation.*

I headed back down the steps. "Here you go." I placed the envelope in her hand.

"Okay, I'll take care of this first thing in the morning." She stood up to leave. "You got big plans for this weekend?"

"Just one thing on my agenda so far."

"Really? What's that?"

"Having dinner with you tomorrow night."

Chapter 18
"In My Bed"

—Dru Hill

My team gave me a nice birthday/Valentine's Day party. I was used to the joint event; it had been that way my entire life.

As I was carrying my gifts to the car, my cell phone rang. "What's up, *D*?" I answered.

"Koby, what's happening? You leaving work?"

"Yeah, I'm about to pull out of the parking lot right now."

"Swing by here, a'ight."

"On my way."

I pulled up to the dealership and spoke to Larry as I headed to Dorian's office.

He stood as I walked in. "The birthday boy in the flesh!"

"And you know this, man." I did the "Harlem shake," and he burst out laughing.

"Chrys made it in yet?"

"Naw, she's not coming."

"That's too bad. Well, you wanna hang out for old times' sake tonight, old man?"

"Dorian, I am exactly six months older than you—who are you calling old? And no, I have plans for the evening."

"What plans? With who?"

I avoided looking at him. "Why you gotta be so nosy?"

"Because you have the tendency to be stupid at times, and I have to be the voice of wisdom, reality, and good sense when this occurs." He leaned against his desk and glared. "You can't even look at me, so I know this must not be kosher. What's up, Koby?"

"Nothing, man. Look, Chrys is with her sick mother and being comforted by her *ex-husband* and it's *my* birthday. I am going out to dinner with Rhea, as friends; there is nothing wrong with that."

"Koby, what are you talking about?" He went and sat in his chair.

I told him about what I overheard on the phone. I explained that Rhea and I had hung out for her birthday and had been talking on the phone.

"That's who you were with the other week at Jernigan's?"

"Yeah. I actually had a good time. It's different this time, *D*. We are really just friends."

"Did you ask her why he was there, or what was up with that?"

"No, and I'm not going to."

"But, Koby, you love Chrys, don't you?"

"I don't even know anymore. I just don't think I can deal with it. I just want to chill."

"So now you're afraid of commitment? That's

what you're trying to say, that this is too much work, so you're quitting?"

"*D*, I'm leaving. I gotta go and get ready. I will see you tomorrow night. We are still going out, right? And tell Jackie she'd better be rolling with us because it's my birthday."

"A'ight, Koby. Man, I hope you know what you're doing."

"I do."

"Keep acting stupid, and you won't be saying those two words at the altar."

"Peace, *D*."

My phone began to vibrate on my hip. I knew it was Chrys. I checked the message: WE NEED TO TALK. CALL ME, PLEASE!

I hit the letters *OK later* and hit the send button.

I decided to concentrate on my evening with Rhea. I planned to go to the Jazz House for dinner and maybe hit a club later for drinks and dancing. I hoped she was down for that.

I carefully chose my attire for the evening, settling on a laid-back, casual look. I dressed in a black and gray Sean John sweater and black jeans and boots. I wore Versace cologne and completed my outfit with the earrings Chrys gave me for Christmas. I opted to leave my phone at home in order to not be distracted by Chrys while I was out. I grabbed my keys and was off to pick up my date.

Rhea was dazzling as usual when she opened her door. Decked out in a cream sweater and matching pants, her stiletto cream boots added about two and a half inches to her small 5-4 frame. Her hair was still longer than I had ever seen her wear it, and her makeup looked professionally applied. She wore classic gold hoops in her petite ears.

"You look so nice, Koby."

"You don't look bad yourself; I am really feeling your hair."

"You like it long? I'm thinking about cutting it again."

"No, leave it like that."

"Well, you ready?"

"Yeah, I thought we'd go to the Jazz House and then hit a club to get our dance on."

"Hey, it's your birthday—whatever you wanna do, I'm down for."

The Cajun food was off the hook. We laughed and talked and had a great dinner. I couldn't remember Rhea ever being like this before. It was as if she was a different person. Our conversation was enjoyable, and we talked about everything from music to politics.

Most of the time, Rhea only focused on herself and what she felt and wanted. Now, it was as if she was just as interested in my thoughts as she was in her own.

Maybe, I misjudged her, I thought to myself. *Maybe I should've given her a second chance.*

"Okay, it's after ten. If we are gonna hit the club, we'd better leave now because it is too cold to be standing in a line," Rhea remarked after we had dessert.

"Well, let's roll out!" I went to grab the check.

"Don't you dare! It's your birthday—my treat."

She paid the waiter, and we continued our evening at the club.

"Wow! I'm impressed—Rhea Davidson paying for someone else!"

She smiled. "The more you give, the more you'll have."

"And you're philosophical now?"

"Let's just say, I've matured." She winked at me.

Luckily, we made it there just as the line was forming and didn't have to wait long. Rhea even paid our way into the club.

"Do you want to get a table or sit at the bar?" She spoke loud enough for me to hear over the music.

"I wanna get my dance on!" I grabbed her and pulled her to the dance floor.

"Then let's go!"

We tore the dance floor up as the DJ pumped Missy's "Get Your Freak On" with some old-school house music.

When the intro to Faith's "I Love You" began to play, Rhea turned to leave, and I pulled her back.

She looked at me with surprise. "But you don't like to slow-dance."

"I've matured." I smiled and held her close.

We spent what seemed like hours on the floor. Eventually, we found a table in the back of the crowded club.

"What are you drinking?" she asked as the waitress came by our table.

"Cognac Paradise," I said without fail.

She paid for our drinks, and we relaxed and joked about other couples.

After a while, I looked over at her and said, "I'm drunk!"

"I know. You ready to go?" She laughed at me.

"You've gotta drive," I slurred.

"I know." She went and got our coats, and we headed to my car.

She drove to my house and helped me to front door. I don't know how we made it into the house, but we did.

"I had so much fun, Rhea. This was the bomb. Thanks."

"I'm glad you did, Koby. I have really missed you," she said as she fumbled with the keys.

We looked at each other and laughed.

"You're drunk too." I giggled.

"No, I don't get drunk. I get *nice*." She laughed back at me.

"How *nice* of you."

We stood there in front of my house, laughing at each other. I know if my neighbors would've looked out at that point they would've called the police.

Once inside, I took off my jacket and lay back on the sofa. I felt her climb on top of me and lay her head on my chest. I looked down at her and began to breathe heavily as she caressed my neck. She eased her way up, and soon we were face to face.

I closed my eyes as I saw her face approaching mine. I parted my lips and felt her mouth on mine. I remembered her taste and began to get aroused, thinking of her.

She sat up and took her sweater off.

I placed my hand on her small breasts. She

pushed my hand down farther and placed it in her pants. I maneuvered my fingers until they found her wetness. She began to moan, her eyes never leaving mine as I played with her.

When I stopped and stood up, she began to look down at the floor. I took her by the hand and led her upstairs to the bedroom.

The next morning I woke up groggy as hell. I groaned, thinking of the night before and what had transpired.

"Good morning. Happy birthday!"

I heard the voice coming up the stairs. I looked down at the sleeping body next to me and sat up confused.

At that moment a figure walked through my open bedroom door. I couldn't even cover Rhea's naked body in order for her not to see it.

"Damn!" was all she said as she looked at the two of us in bed together. She turned and ran down the steps.

I heard my front door open, and all of a sudden a crash came through my front window.

I jumped out of the bed and rushed to see what it was. There lying on the floor next to Rhea's sweater was Chrys' Blackberry. I picked it up and knew that this was one of those situations that Momma was talking about.

"Rhea." I shook her gently.

"What? My head." She moaned, rolled over on her stomach, and buried her head under a pillow.

"Come on, Rhea, get up."

"God, Koby, I feel terrible. What time is it?"

I looked over at the clock, unsure of the time myself. "It's nine-fifteen." *Think*, I said to myself. *Calm down and get it together.* It didn't help that my head was banging and my mouth felt like I had been eating cotton sandwiches.

I went into the bathroom and threw some cold water on my face. I looked up and saw my reflection in the mirror. *Today is my twenty-eighth birthday and I just ruined one of the best things that ever happened to me.* I quickly brushed my teeth and left out of the bathroom because the more I looked at myself, the more disgusted I became.

I could hear Rhea talking and when I went into the room, I found her sitting on the side of the bed on the phone. "Hold on. Here he is." She passed me the phone.

It took all I had not to ask who gave her permission to answer my phone; instead, I just took it from her. My heart was pounding as I thought about who was on the other end. "Hello."

"Well, I don't have to wonder how your dinner with your *friend* went," Dorian said, his voice dripping with sarcasm.

"What's up, Dorian?"

"Just called to tell you happy birthday, Koby. I can see that you got company this morning though."

"Thanks, *D*. Look, I'm on my way over there; I'll see you in a few minutes."

Rhea turned and frowned at me.

"What's wrong? I thought you were coming over here later?"

"I said I'll see you in a minute, *D*."

"A'ight, Koby, but don't bring her over here; it's too early in the morning for me to listen to Jackie going off! I'll see you when you get here, and bring some Krispy Kreme," he yelled as he hung up the phone.

"Koby, you're going over to Dorian's *now*?" Rhea looked confused.

"Yeah, I'm sorry, Rhea, but I got some stuff I gotta take care of this morning." I handed her a washcloth so she could wash up.

While she was in the bathroom, I ran downstairs to get her sweater.

"You wanna hook up later, Koby?" she asked me as she got dressed.

"I don't know, Rhea. I told you I got some stuff to take care of today."

"But it's Valentine's Day!" she whined and put her arms around my waist.

She didn't even mention my birthday. "I know. Come on, I gotta go and meet Dorian."

We descended down the steps, and I got our coats.

She hollered, seeing the broken glass, "What happened to your window?"

"Somebody threw a rock or something this morning," I mumbled and passed her jacket.

"You don't seem to be mad about it. Aren't you even gonna pick the glass up?" She kneeled down and started picking up the pieces. "Go get the broom."

"Leave it; I'll get it later." I remembered I left my cell lying on my dresser. I wanted it just in case Chrys decided to call, although, deep down, I knew she wouldn't.

While we were riding in the car, Rhea asked, "Why are you so quiet?"

"I just got a lot on my mind."

She glanced over at me. "Are you mad about last night?"

"No, I'm not mad; I had a nice time."

She opened her door and looked at me as she got out of the car. "No compromise, no regret, Koby. I don't regret last night, because I didn't have to compromise our friendship. I will always care for you, no matter what. Call me later." She leaned over and kissed my cheek.

"Yeah."

"Happy birthday and Happy Valentine's Day!" She unlocked her door and went into her house.

After picking up the Krispy Kreme that Dorian requested, I checked my cell phone. I realized that I had messages waiting. I pulled into his driveway and sat in the car while I checked my voicemail:

Hi, Koby. It's midnight and I wanted to be the first one to wish you happy birthday. This is also a Valentine's Day wish as well, to my one true love. No one has ever given so much of his self and his time, let alone his heart, to me, and I love you for that. Happy birthday, baby. I have a special gift for you that is scheduled for delivery at about nine in the morning, so please be ready to sign for it. I think you'll really like it. I'll talk to you later. I love you.

I lay my head into the steering wheel and let the cell phone drop to the seat.

"You got my Krispy Kreme?" Dorian was peeping into my window. He opened the back door and removed the two boxes of doughnuts. "I hope you got some cream-filled too. Come on, so you can tell me how you messed up."

I reluctantly got out of the car and followed him into the house.

Jackie was just about to leave with the girls, who were all dressed in pink dance attire. "Happy birthday, Koby." She gave me a hug, and a kiss on the cheek.

"Happy birthday, Uncle Koby!" All three girls ran and hugged me.

"Thank you, sweeties!" I kissed each one as they headed out the door.

"Ooh, Krispy Kreme! We'll be back by five." Jackie reached into the box and grabbed a doughnut.

Dorian and I went into the kitchen. He got two tall glasses out of the cabinet, filled one with milk, and the other with ice and ginger ale. He reached on top of the refrigerator and passed me two aspirin along with the soda.

"Well," he said, "I know you got some, and you must've got drunk, because you're hung over. But something else had to happen and it must be big, because you drove across town to get me some doughnuts and didn't complain once!"

"I messed up. I really messed up."

"This I know. You screwed Rhea, didn't you?" He licked the doughnut glaze off his fingers.

"No, stupid, I didn't do anything like that."

"Then what are you talking about? Can you fill me in?" He drank half his milk and reached for another doughnut.

I told him about dinner and the club and how

much fun Rhea and I had. I explained that we got drunk and wound up sleeping together at my house. Then I dropped the news that Chrys showed up at my house this morning.

"Wow! Did she know Rhea was upstairs?"

I shook my head. "She came up the stairs and caught us in bed together."

"Damn!"

"Her words exactly—Then she jetted out the door and threw her phone through my front window."

"What did Rhea do?"

"Nothing. She slept through the whole thing. I had to wake her up to leave."

"Oh"—Dorian took a deep breath—"So now what are you going to do?"

"I don't know what to do. I messed up, I told you; I just want to fix it."

"This one is gonna be hard to fix, Koby; I can't even help you with this one. This isn't some innocent little, finding-a-number-in-your-pocket type thing. Exactly what did she see?"

"Put it this way—Rhea and I both were butt naked *on top* of the covers."

"You can't even say that y'all just fell asleep."

"I don't even want to try something like that; I respect her too much to lie."

"Let me be the devil's advocate here—you respect her too much to lie, but you don't respect her enough to *not* sleep with your ex-girlfriend—And you call me stupid?"

"*D*, what am I gonna do?"

"You try to call her? How about going over there?"

"No, I just came straight here."

"I'm telling you right now—she's not going to want to hear anything you have to say."

"I know. That's one reason I didn't call—I know she's mad."

"'Mad'? You think she's mad? Boy, you have no idea."

"*D*, I love her."

"I know, Koby, but this is gonna be a hard one."

"I don't care how hard it is."

"It's gonna take some time."

"I don't care how long it takes."

He handed me the phone. "Then get to work."

I dialed Chrys' number, and as I suspected, she didn't answer.

I said goodbye to Dorian and drove to her house, but her car was gone. I used my key and let myself in. There were no suitcases or bags in the living room, so I went into her room. There were pieces of clothes scattered on her bed. I walked over to her closet and pulled the sliding doors open—all of her clothes were gone!

I took one final look around and reluctantly left. I drove around the city for the remainder of the day, hoping to possibly run into her, calling her cell phone every thirty minutes hoping she might pick up by accident. I never felt so bad in my life.

I climbed in bed too depressed to even think. *Happy birthday to me.*

I left a message for her on her cell phone a week later after I couldn't get in contact with her:

Chrys, baby, I am so sorry. I know that is the last thing you want to hear right now. And I also know that there is nothing I can say to change what happened. I love you and I want to talk to you. Please at least call me to let me know you're okay. Please. I love you so much. Call me.

Two days later, I came home from work, looked on the caller ID, and saw the Georgia area code. She left this message:

It's Chryslin. I allowed you the courtesy of this phone call to let you know that I am alive and well. I am sorry that things didn't work out between us, and you're right—there is nothing you can say. You're no better than he was, and you have no regard for me or my feelings, obviously, or it never would've happened. You couldn't have loved me, or you wouldn't have done what you did. She began to sob. *Goodbye, Koby.*

Chapter 19

"I'm a Mess"

—Anthony Hamilton

Eventually, the hurt that I felt about Chrys turned to numbness. I betrayed her, and her ex-husband had probably used it as an opportunity for them to reconcile. He was there for her, when her mom was sick, and they already were married; it worked out for the best. I had settled for hoping that she was happy.

"Team meeting in ten minutes, Koby," Ms. Juanita said, snapping me back to reality.

"Thanks, Ms. Juanita. I'll be there." I grabbed the itinerary for my mid-monthly staff meeting and headed to the conference room.

"You okay?"

I smiled. "Yeah, I was just thinking about something."

The meeting went well. I announced the goals for the upcoming months and concluded by commending my team on a job well done.

At the end of the meeting, Brenda walked over to me and asked if everything was all right.

"Yeah, I'm fine."

"I know you're distracted. Does this have anything with to do with Chrys leaving?—I know you all were seeing each other on the *DL*. And today when she came and cleared her desk, I was surprised too."

"Chrys was here? Today?"

"Yeah, she should still be upstairs."

"I'll be right back." I opted to run up the stairs, rather than catch the elevator. I rushed to Chrys' desk, only to find everything gone.

I went to Phil Barnes' office. "Hey, Phil, do you know where Chrys Matthews is?"

"She just left. She decided to come and get all of her stuff because she is taking a full leave of absence."

"I know her mother is ill, but I thought she was getting better."

"I guess not. She's transferring to the Atlanta office."

"Thanks, Phil." I went back down to my desk and grabbed my things. I told Brenda I had an emergency and had to leave.

I made it to Chrys' house in twelve minutes flat, where her car was hooked to the back of a U-Haul.

She came out of her house carrying a box. She stopped dead in her tracks when she saw me. "What do you want?" she said fiercely.

I looked down and didn't know what to say. I shook my head and took a deep breath. "Can I talk to you in private for a moment?"

"What could we possibly have to talk about?"

"I want to apologize for what happened."

"No need; it's over." She brushed past me to the back of the truck.

I turned to face her. "Please, let me explain."

"There is no need to explain." She walked past me again.

"Chrys . . ." I reached for her arm.

"Don't touch me! Just leave me alone."

"Hold up, man!" A guy came out of the house and walked over to where we were talking.

"Look, I know this is your wife and I'm not trying to be disrespectful, but I really need to talk her in private."

"Leave it alone, Tony. Go ahead inside; I can handle him." She motioned for him to go into the house.

"Nice to meet you, my brother. Don't keep my *wife* out here too long—we gotta hit the road."

She rolled her eyes at him then looked at me. "Okay, we're alone. Now what is so private?"

"I can't believe you're going back to him. Do you remember he attacked you not too long ago, not to mention his cheating on you? Don't tell me you think he's changed. You're too good for him! I love you!"

"Have you lost your mind? How dare you stand there and lecture me about someone else's infidelities. What I do remember is you fucking your ex-girlfriend while I was breaking my neck to leave my sick mother in order to be with you on your birthday! I do remember her being butt naked in the bed that you and I made love in! So, JaKoby Jackson, please don't give me ill advice on how to deal with my ex because, while you supposedly loved me, you were screwing yours. NOW GET THE HELL OUT OF MY LIFE!"

I turned and walked away from her. It felt as if she stabbed me in me heart. I looked back at her before I got into the car.

Tears were streaming down her face as she watched me leave, and she began to slump over. Tony came out and caught her, and she buried her face in his chest.

"I love you, Chrys," I said before I got in my car.

"The sad point is I loved you too, Koby."

Tony helped her into the house.

I cried all the way home.

"I love my job, Koby!" Jaamell said as he got into the car.

"That's great, *J.* I hope you're doing a good job. You may need a letter of recommendation in the near future and one from the firm would be good."

"You know I'm doing a good job. I learned from you. I get compliments every day on my gear. I am the best-dressed mail clerk there. I dress better that some of the partners." He smiled and loos-ened his tie.

I dropped the top so we could get some air in the already stifling June temperature.

"Cut on some music, Koby. It's Friday, and we 'bout to go kick it with Dorian!" Jaamell changed the radio station and turned the volume up, and Mary J. Blige blared from the speakers.

I quickly turned the station to talk radio.

"What are you doing?—That's my jam!"

"I don't feel like hearing that today, *J.*"

"You never wanna listen to anything but talk radio. What is with you, Koby?"

I didn't want to tell him that I was wallowing in heartbreak and that any song I heard reminded me of the one true love I had. "I just got a lot on my mind these days, *J.* Look, I know you want to have fun this summer, and I am sorry I am dragging you down. I just—"

"Hey, Koby, man, I know you are down about Chrys. I'm sorry she had to move away," he said sincerely. "It's hard for me and Chela, and we're only an hour apart."

I'd told my family that Chrys and I decided that a long-distance relationship wasn't working for us and we were giving it a break until things got settled.

"I know it isn't hard for you two because my phone bill reflects otherwise." I laughed.

Jaamell tried to change the subject. "What are we doing for the Fourth?"

"What do you wanna do? I usually hang out at Dorian's."

"Well, the firm is having a cookout, and I'd really like for us to go. I also wanna bring Chela . . . if we can convince her parents to let her come for the weekend."

"I don't see going to the cookout being a problem. You're on your own with Chela and her parents, though."

"Yeah, I gotta think about that one."

Jaamell's plans to spend Fourth of July weekend with Chela actually worked, once he and Chela advised her parents that she wouldn't be staying with me overnight, but with a mature, well-established, family friend, who was a stable, single woman.

"I don't see what the problem is, Koby," Rhea said, drinking her milkshake.

We'd met at the food court in the mall for lunch one afternoon the week before the Fourth. Somehow, I found myself spending more and more time with Rhea, even though she never pressed the issue of being more than friends, which made it easier for me to enjoy her company. There was no pressure. We would just meet somewhere for dinner or drinks and chill. The discussion of our sleeping together on my birthday never came up. She didn't mention it, and neither did I.

"The problem is that this girl is going to be your responsibility, and if anything happens, it's on you."

"Okay, Koby, I accept full responsibility. You act like I'm irresponsible or something."

I looked at her like she was crazy, and we burst out laughing.

"So I have acted immature at one point or another—that doesn't make me irresponsible."

"Do I need to remind you of a certain someone mooning a famous ex-football player through the sunroof one Christmas Eve?" I nudged her arm.

She squealed. "Did not that same football player moon me first?"

I was hysterical by now.

"You *both* are crazy," I said when I caught my breath.

Rhea smiled affectionately. "It's good to laugh with you again, Koby."

"It's good to laugh again, Rhea. Again, thanks for getting Jaamell the summer job; he really loves it."

"He is a good worker. I'm glad Chela is coming this weekend because I know some of my female *compadres* have their eye on him."

"Do they know he is jailbait?"

"I don't think they care. And on that note, I am out." She gave me a quick hug. "Face it, Koby—your little brother is fine! Must run in the family. See you this weekend." Rhea left me standing there amazed by what she'd said about Jaamell.

Chapter 20

"4 Seasons of Loneliness"

—Boyz II Men

The Sykes, Jones, and Puryear annual Fourth of July picnic was, without question, one heck of a bash. There were the traditional ribs, chicken, hamburger and hotdogs, steaks, potato salad, baked beans, and all the trimmings. But they also had fish, crab, lobster, and an open bar with free flowing champagne and, to top it off a red, white, and blue flag-cake that spanned an entire picnic table.

"Welcome to the big league, boo," Jaamell told Chela as we approached the campground that was rented for the event. There were people playing softball, volleyball, tossing horseshoes, not to mention a magician and clowns for the kids as well as a DJ.

"It may be the big league, but I see they still keep it real. Look at them over there playing spades!" Chela giggled.

"Ha, ha! That's Michael Puryear, my boss and one of the firm's partners," Jaamell announced.

I looked over at the table where Michael was sitting with three women. *Punk ass*! My ego was still slightly bruised when I thought about him and Rhea. "You're not gonna go over and speak to your boy?" I asked Rhea, waiting for her reaction.

She hissed, "Don't try to be funny, Koby."

I couldn't help laughing.

We all had a ball, eating and playing the games and even joining in on the Electric Slide.

Towards the end of the day, Michael came to the microphone and thanked everyone for coming. "Certainly, we appreciate each and every one of our employees, and this barbecue is just one way we try to show our gratitude and enjoy each of you as a family. And as my family, I would like to share a very special moment with you.

As many of you know, this has been a very trying year for me. But there is one person that has been by my side every step of the way. She has come in early and stayed late, working just as hard as I have, dealing with everything that has come our way. She is my right hand, and I have grown to love her very much."

I looked over at Rhea, whose eyes got wide with surprise. Some other people began to look her way.

"So at this time I would like to get on my knees in front of you, my family, and ask Nichole Baldwin if she will do the honor of becoming my wife."

People began to clap and cheer as Nichole screamed and ran up to the front of the crowd.

"That was so beautiful," Chela said. "She must be very special."

"Now *that* was player!" Jaamell clapped and whistled.

I turned to Rhea, who had turned as red as a beet. "Are you okay?" I asked her.

"Yeah, I just need to be alone for a moment," she whispered as she turned and walked away.

I waited a few moments and then went behind her. I found her sitting beside her car with her head in her arms. "Hey, mind if I join you?"

"Karma is a bitch, huh?" she said, her eyes red from crying.

"What do you mean?" I put my arm around her.

"I mean what goes around comes around."

"I don't believe in karma."

She sniffled. "Believe it. I cheated on you with him, and he cheated on me with her—karma."

"I think that's just him being a ho."

"Then why is he marrying her and not still ho'in'? Why didn't he stop with me and marry me. Face it, it's Karma."

"Who's to say he's gonna stop after he gets married?—Once a 'ho', always a 'ho'!" I tried to make her smile.

"Nice try, Koby. Maybe I'm not the marrying type. Maybe guys don't see me as wife material."

"Well, you sure as hell can't cook, and I definitely can't see you with no kids, that's for sure."

"You're certainly not helping me right now." She put her head back in her arms.

"Come on, get up. I refuse to let you wallow in self-pity. Now let's go up to the happy couple and congratulate them."

"Why would I want to do that, Koby?"

"Because, number one, he's your boss, and she's your co-worker, and number two, to show that you're over both of them because they deserve

each other—karma—you'd want her to congratulate you."

"I thought you didn't believe in karma?"

"I don't, but it's still the right thing to do. You
said you believe in karma, so you'd better be nice
to them so something good will come out of it for
you. Now come on." I pulled her up and wiped her
face. I began to laugh out loud.

"What's so funny?" she asked.

"You, with some kids, cooking dinner—imagine
that."

She turned to me and flipped the bird, with a
smile on her face.

"I need a favor," Rhea said to me the Friday before Labor Day.

We were still doing the "friend" thing, since I'd
made sure to not put us in any compromising po-
sitions.

"What?"

"Okay, you know Charisse and Jeff are getting
married in December. Hell, everyone is getting
married except for me."

"I'm not getting married yet."

"Precisely—*yet*. Anyway, they are having an engagement party/barbecue on Monday. Can you
please go with me?"

"Rhea, I was gonna hang at Dorian's for Labor
Day. I didn't even go over there for Fourth of July."

"Koby, you were just over there night before last;
you act like you never get to see them or something. Please . . . I have to go to this because I'm
her maid of honor. Don't make me go by myself."

"But my parents are staying at Dorian's for the weekend, and Jaamell is staying with me."

"Quit whining. Okay, we don't have to stay for the entire thing. I will make a quick appearance, and then we can leave. Please, Koby? I need you to do this for me."

"Oh, now who's whining? A'ight, Rhea, I will give you two hours, and then I'm out."

"Thank you, thank you, thank you." She kissed me through the phone. "You said something good would come out of me congratulating that heifer Nichole and her dog of a fiancé, Michael—karma!"

"Whatever. I was thinking more in line of your ass getting a raise when I said that."

On Monday we arrived at the party just as it was getting good. I congratulated Jeff and Charisse and told them how happy I was for them.

"I'm glad to hear you say that, Koby, because I would like for you to be a groomsman."

"A what?" I almost choked.

"I know I kind of caught you off guard, but I need another one with all of these bridesmaids Charisse has. I know we aren't that close, but I would be honored if you would."

"I mean-I-if you want me to, I don't have a problem with it."

"See, I told you he'd do it." Rhea looped her arm through mine and kissed me on my cheek.

At that moment a well-built man looking very much like Jeff walked up. "Well, if it isn't Rhea Davidson," he said. "Andre. Andre Young, Jeff's brother." He extended his hand.

"Koby Jackson. Pleased to meet you."

We exchanged small talk, and then he left to speak to some other guests.

I turned to Rhea. "Wow! I didn't know Jeff had a brother. Are they twins?"

"No. Andre is two years older." Rhea frowned. "He doesn't live here anymore."

"Oh, why didn't you tell me Jeff wanted me to be in the wedding? I felt kind of uncomfortable."

"It was last-minute. Charisse had more brides-maids than groomsmen, and they needed to even it out. She asked me, and I told her it probably wouldn't be a problem because I would probably bring you as my date anyway. Come on, let's get some food."

We hung around for another hour, and then I motioned to Rhea it was time to go.

As we were leaving, Andre came over and shook my hand once again. "Hey, Jeff told me you agreed to be a groomsman. I'll let you know when the bachelor party is gonna be."

"Definitely keep me filled in. It was nice meeting you." I nodded at him.

"Same here. Rhea, nice seeing you again." He kissed her on the cheek.

"He is real cool; I like him," I said as we were leaving.

She shrugged. "Yeah, he's a'ight, I guess."

Chapter 21

"Anytime"

—Brian McKnight

When we arrived at Dorian's, Rhea hesitated to get out of the car. She sat staring out of the window. "Jackie hates me; I don't want to be here."

"Jackie does not hate you," I lied; "she's just got to get to know you."

"Please don't make me stay here long. I want you to enjoy your family, and you can't do that while I'm here."

"Rhea, come on, it will be fine." I walked around and opened the door to let her out.

We walked around to the back of the house, where we found Jaamell, Chela, and Dorian and the girls indulging themselves in the pool. Pops and Uncle Theodore were manning the grill, and Jackie and Momma were sitting, enjoying a pitcher of margaritas.

"Hey, look who made it," Dorian announced as we came through the back gate.

"Hi, baby. Hello, Rhea." Momma rose to hug both of us.

"Hey, Ma." I kissed her on the cheek. "What's up, everybody?"

Everyone said their hellos, and Rhea and I went to sit at the table with Jackie.

"How're you doing, Rhea?" Jackie asked, surprising both of us.

"I'm fine, Jackie," she said quietly. How have you been?"

Jackie and Momma made a little more small talk, and everyone eventually loosened up a bit.

A little while later, Rhea excused herself and went to the restroom.

"Thanks, Jackie. I really appreciate your being nice."

"Shut up, Koby. I'm only doing it because Chela told us she had changed and wasn't stuck up anymore, not that I believe it. I still don't trust her, and you'd better watch your back."

"Both of y'all need to shut up because here she comes," Momma whispered.

"Well, I hate to be rude, but I have to be going," Rhea said as she returned to the table.

"What's wrong, Rhea? You're not sick, are you?" Momma asked.

"No, ma'am. I just have a migraine. Koby, if you want to stay, I can call a cab."

"Nonsense. I can take you."

We said our goodbyes and went to the car.

"What's wrong? I thought it was going okay in there. Why you wanna leave so soon?"

"I told you I would catch a cab if it was a problem, Koby. I really don't feel well."

"No, it's all good. I'll take you home."

We rode to her house in silence.

"You sure you're gonna be okay?" I asked as she got out. "I can walk you to the door."

"I'm fine. I just need to go get in the bed. I know you're not trying to join me," she said with a weak smile.

"No, but it was worth a try. I'll check on you later."

"Thanks, Koby. I appreciate today. I had fun." She got out, and I made sure she got into the house.

It was early fall, and I still couldn't stop thinking about Chryslin Matthews. I couldn't get her out of my mind. I doubted if I could ever love someone as much as I loved her. It had gotten to the point where she began to haunt me in my dreams.

"I told you it would take some time," Dorian said in an effort to comfort me one night when we'd decided to meet at Jernigan's for a drink.

"I thought you meant it would take time for us to get back together. I didn't know you were talking about getting over her." I looked down into my drink.

"Well, at the time I thought you would be able to get back together. Time heals all wounds, nevertheless."

I looked down at the other end of the bar and noticed a familiar face. "Jeff?"

The man looked up. "No, man, it's Dre." He smiled feebly.

"I'm sorry, Dre; you all could pass for twins. Come on down here and join us. Dorian, this is Jeff's brother, Andre."

He came and sat between Dorian and me.

"How you doing? Man, y'all do look alike." Dorian extended his hand.

"What's wrong, Dre?" I asked. "You look like I feel?"

"Bartender, another round for my poor, depressed brothers over here!" Dorian yelled.

"My wife gave birth to a 6-pound, 4-ounce baby girl today, and I wasn't there."

"Man, how the hell did you miss that?" Dorian asked.

"She really didn't want me to be there anyway." Dre sighed. "I messed things up a long time ago."

"Yeah, you do need a drink," I told him.

We shared a few more rounds, while watching the last few innings of the Mets game.

"Fellas, I gotta roll," Dre said an hour later. "Thanks for the drinks. And hey, don't forget about Jeff's bachelor party. Dorian, you're invited too," he yelled as he walked out the door.

"I guess I'm not the only one who messed up, huh?" I said after he was gone.

"Koby, I know you loved Chrys, but, maybe it's time to move on. I'm not saying forget about her, but move on to something else."

"Okay, maybe you're right," I said, but deep down, my heart still ached.

"Are you ready to be escorted by the greatest of all time?" I asked Rhea when she opened her front door. It was Halloween and Jackie had decided to throw a costume party for Dorian's birthday.

"Why, Mr. Ali, is that a banana in your boxers, or are you happy to see me?" She stood back and admired my costume, which consisted of full boxing gear, and a silk robe with *Ali* stitched across the back.

"My, my, my, do you do windows, madame?" I checked out her perfect body in the black and white French maid's costume. "Um, makes me wanna stay here and clean the house." I pulled her to me and kissed her full on the mouth.

Upon taking Dorian's advice, I decided that maybe I could give Rhea and me another chance, and she was more than willing to agree. We had been doing okay too.

"Come on, Muhammad, let's go before your business starts poking through your costume." Rhea grabbed her coat.

"You make me rise to the occasion, baby." I hit her on her behind as we left out.

Our physical relationship was on an all-time high. Once we got to the party, she even suggested we go upstairs; it was as if Rhea couldn't get enough of me. I happily obliged.

We took the steps all the way to the third floor of Dorian's house and walked into his private office. I led Rhea to the French doors and opened them. We walked outside to the balcony overlooking the sprawling back yard.

Rhea led me to the edge of the balcony and positioned herself in front of me. "This is so gorgeous," she said.

"You are too." I began sucking her neck.

She reached under my robe and rubbed me until I really was sticking through my shorts. She bent slightly over the balcony and put my hands under her short skirt.

"Oh, my, is this a G-string?" I said in a loud whisper.

She laughed and spread her legs apart slightly. "Easy access, baby."

She moaned as I entered her from behind.

When we joined the rest of the party, Jackie whispered in my ear, "You'd better watch yourself, Koby. I still don't trust her—once a trick, always a trick. She's just treating you right, right now."

I brushed her off, and she marched away looking like a crazed Elvira.

"What's her deal?" Rhea asked me, seeing the whole thing.

"Nothing. She's just worried about me. It's all good."

"You know, Koby, if she was really worried, she'd see that I make you happy and be satisfied with that. You'd better check her before I do."

"Come on, Rhea, don't be like that. She loves me and wants nothing but the best for me."

"Then she should know that I'm as good as it gets." Rhea rolled her eyes at Jackie and kissed me boldly.

I decided we'd better leave while the getting was good.

Chapter 22

"Share My World"

—Mary J. Blige

Andre called me two weeks later to give me the info on Jeff's bachelor party. I assured him that Dorian and I would be there on Saturday night. Andre rented a private party room on the top floor of the Clarion Hotel. Five strippers of different sizes, shapes and colors entertained us and about twenty-five of Jeff's friends. We whooped and hollered as Jeff was treated to some delightful pleasures by each one.

At the end of the evening we were each given a hat made out of thongs, and a T-shirt with the words *I survived Jeff's Bachelor Party* emblazoned on the front.

"Thank you, guys, for coming," Andre said as Dorian and I got ready to leave.

"No. Thanks for inviting us. Man, when I get married I want you to plan my party," I told him.

"Just let me know the date, and I will hook you up, man."

"Hey, did you get everything straight with your situation?" Dorian asked him.

"Huh?" Dre looked confused.

"The situation you were telling us about at the bar."

"Oh, *that* situation." Dre laughed. "Yeah, she'll be at the wedding; that's a start."

"That's a *good* start," I responded. "You know how women are at weddings."

The beautiful Puerto Rican stripper came up behind him. "Dre, baby, are we still on for tonight?"

"What? Oh, yeah, well, I gotta go take care of her. I'll see you guys in three weeks at the wedding."

Dorian and I looked at each other.

"If he's all about getting back with his wife," I whispered, "why is he taking care of her?"

"He probably meant pay her, man; that's stripper talk," Dorian, now slightly drunk, said matter-of-factly.

I laughed. "I didn't know they had a special code."

The next day, Rhea came over and got in bed with me. While we were cuddling, she asked, "How was the party?"

"It was good."

"Were there a lot of strippers?" She looked at me.

"I don't know."

"What was Jeff doing?"

"Rhea, it is a code between men—what goes on at the bachelor party, stays at the bachelor party."

"Well, did you have fun?"

"I'm not answering any more questions."

"Koby, I have something to tell you." She looked at me funny.

"What?—you had a camera hidden somewhere at the party last night?"

"No. I'm pregnant," she said barely above a whisper.

I thought I misunderstood her. "You're what?"

"I said, 'I'm pregnant.'"

"I thought you were getting the shot and it was 99% effective?"

"I was, but I took it late the other month and my doctor said I was still gonna be okay. Obviously she was wrong."

"Obviously. What do you want to do, Rhea?"

"I want to get married."

"Get what?"

"Married. But I know that isn't going to happen. So, whatever you want to do, I'm cool with it."

I closed my eyes and thought about everything that I had been through this past year—Rhea, grad school, my new job, Chrys, everything. Then I thought of my family—Momma, Pop, Jaamell, Dorian, Jackie—and everything I believed in. God had been good to me. And maybe this was His way of blessing me with the wife and child I had been praying for my entire life.

I looked at her. "Then we'll get married."

"Do you mean it?" She started to cry.

"I mean it," I said, hoping I knew what I was doing.

She screamed and kissed me.

* * *

On Thanksgiving evening, after the entire family had retired to the den to listen to Pop and Uncle Theodore, I told everyone I had an announcement.

"I, first of all, want to thank each of you for being a special part of my life. I can't think of any better time than to do this in front of the people I love. Rhea, can you please come here."

She walked over to me, and I put my arm around her.

She whispered, "Get on your knee!"

"Let me do this my way!" I whispered back. "I love you, Rhea, and I want to make you my wife. Will you marry me?"

The entire family looked as if they were frozen. Out of the corner of my eye, I could see Dorian holding Jackie down.

"Of course, Koby!" Rhea said loudly.

I removed the ring from the front pocket of my shirt and placed it on her finger.

"Congratulations, son." Pop gave me a hug as Rhea went to show her new ring off to Momma and Chela.

"Thanks, Pop. I appreciate it."

Momma walked over to me and hugged me. "Did you pray about this, Koby?" She looked at me.

I knew I couldn't lie. "Of course. I thought about this, Ma. I love her." I decided to keep the news about the pregnancy to myself. I didn't want them to think that was the only reason I proposed.

"I didn't ask if you *thought* about it. You need to *pray* about it, Koby."

"She's right, Koby," Dorian said from behind me. "You have to do more than think about this one, but I want you to know, whatever you do, your family is behind you one hundred percent, like we always have been."

"Thanks, *D.*"

We all had a group hug.

"Jackie okay?"

"She will be; just let her know that you're happy—that is the most important thing to her."

I walked into the kitchen, where she was putting away the food. "What's up, Jackie Chan?"

"Chillin', Koby. You want some of this food to take home?"

"I'll get some later."

"Well, I know how much your *fiancée* likes Momma Jackson's peach cobbler and pound cake, so I'll be sure to pack her some." She wiped the tears from her face.

"Jackie, please stop."

"Just let me say this, Koby—I've told you time and time again that you are one of the good guys and you deserve someone special. I can't pick that person for you; all I can do is love you and hope that you end up happy. Now, regardless of the fact that she is *supposedly* pregnant, until you can look me in my face and tell me that *she* truly makes you happy, then please don't expect me to be happy for you."

I hugged her and told her that I loved her too.

Chapter 23

"If I Ain't Got You"

—Alicia Keys

"You ready to do this?" I asked Jeff.

He looked like he wanted to throw up. "Yeah. I hear you're next." He wiped his brow with his handkerchief.

Andre joined us. "Really? That's great, Koby. Who is the lucky girl?"

"Rhea," I told him.

"Rhea Davidson?" He blinked at me and tilted his head.

"Yeah, we're having a baby."

He and Jeff stopped to look at me in amazement.

"Wow!" Jeff looked at Dre funny. "Charisse didn't tell me she was pregnant."

I tried to break the tension that had suddenly filled the room. "Hey, did your wife make it?"

"Yeah, she should be here."

"You excited?"

"Yeah. I'm really gonna try and get her back."

"Well, good luck; I hope everything works out for you."

"You too, Koby."

The wedding director came and told us, "Time to take your places."

Jeff and Charisse's wedding was a beautiful event. The church was packed, and I could feel myself getting nervous as I marched with Rhea down the aisle. We glanced at each other throughout the ceremony, and she began to cry during their vows. I had to smile at her.

I was glad when it was all over, but then we took pictures for forty-five minutes. By the time we left for the reception, we were famished.

"I am starving," Rhea said as we waited for the bridal party to be announced. She lifted her hand to admire the one and a half carat engagement ring I presented her with on Thanksgiving Day.

"You like your ring?"

"I *love* my ring!"

"You like your man?"

"I *love* my man!" She gave me a big kiss. "I am going straight home after the reception because I am so tired." She feigned a yawn.

"You mean you don't want to hang out with your friends for a while?"

"No, but if you want to stay for a minute, you can."

Finally we were announced and took our seats at the head table. We ate dinner as the couple took their first dance and the reception really kicked off when the DJ began playing Michael Jackson's "P.Y.T."

I was standing at the bar when I heard someone tap me on the shoulder. I turned around and stared into the most beautiful face I could ever remember seeing in my life. "Chrys!"

"Hello, Koby," she said, tears beginning to form in her eyes.

"What are you doing here?" I asked.

"Jeff is—well—*was* my brother-in-law."

"What?"

As we stood staring at each other, Dre walked up. "You two know each other?"

I tried to swallow. "I'm a manager at the telephone company."

"Oh, that's nice. And this is little Miss Jamila. Say hi, baby." Andre reached into the stroller I hadn't noticed before.

I looked at the cocoa-colored infant with the head full of hair and stared straight into the eyes of my great-grandmother. "God, she's beautiful!" I exclaimed.

"That's what her name means," Andre informed me.

"Yo, Dre!" someone yelled across the room.

"I'll be back. You all go ahead and catch up."

"You wanna go talk in the lobby?" I said slowly.

"Yeah, that's a good idea," Chrys replied.

I grabbed the stroller and pushed it out to the lobby, where we found a quiet spot to sit.

"She's mine, isn't she? I know she is." I lifted my beautiful daughter out of the stroller and laughed when I noticed the earrings I gave Chrys for

Christmas in her ears and then noticed Chrys was wearing the matching pendant. My heart began to leap with joy when I held her on my shoulder and she began to nuzzle me.

"I knew the eyes would be a dead giveaway. I was gonna tell you, but then I heard you got back with Rhea . . . in more ways than one. Congratulations on your engagement."

"I heard you were reconciling your marriage."

"Well, that one you definitely heard wrong."

I looked down at my beautiful daughter in her mother's arms. "But he really wants to make it work."

"He thinks he wants to make it work; he doesn't know what he wants."

"He must have gotten a little bit of what he wanted . . . because he thinks my baby is his."

"I slept with him one night in a moment of weakness after I moved back to Atlanta. He came to visit and I was still so angry at you. Let's see just how bad he wants to get back with me"—She reached in the diaper bag and took out a cell phone.

"Who are you calling?" I asked.

"I'm seeing just how much he wants to make this work." She dialed some numbers and hit speaker-phone.

I shook my head and laughed. "Old habits die hard, huh?"

Sorry I can't take your call right now—I recognized Dre's voice immediately this time.

She hit a series of numbers, and all of a sudden a familiar voice came through the speaker:

Dre, it's me, Rhea. You know I am trying to get some of that after the wedding. You worked me out so well last week that I'm ready for it again. Call me as soon as you get rid of your ex-wife for the evening. I've already planned my excuse. Let me know where you wanna meet.

We sat and looked at each other, neither one saying a word.

Epilogue

"Forever Mine"

—The O'Jays

I had never been so nervous in my life. I looked at my wife lying in the hospital bed, her face covered in sweat. It had been a long night, and I knew she was tired. I reached over on the nightstand, got a cool washcloth, and wiped her forehead.

"It's another one," she moaned and clenched the side of the bed. Her contractions were about a minute apart now.

I knew that, in moments, I would be holding a new baby in my arms. "Breathe, honey." I grabbed her hands.

The door opened, and her doctor stepped in. "You ready, Mrs. Jackson?"

"I've been ready," she cried. "I gotta push!"

Before I knew it, I was holding one leg, and her mother was holding the other—she was giving birth right before my eyes.

Dorian had been teasing me over the past nine

months that I was going to either be fainting from the sight or bawling like a two-year-old.

I told him he was wrong on both accounts.

As I watched the head emerge, my eyes began to swell with tears, and I realized he was right. "Push, baby, push."

She yelled. "I'm pushing!"

"Well, well, well, it's a boy!" the doctor announced.

I leaned over and put my forehead against hers. "I love you so much, baby. Thank you."

"Dad, you wanna cut the cord?"

I carefully cut the cord and watched as they wrapped my baby in blankets. His cry was like music to my ears.

"Seven pounds, three ounces," the nurse said, a few seconds later, and passed him to us.

"He's beautiful." I kissed his forehead.

My wife laughed. "He looks like his dad."

"Jealous?" I asked.

"Uh, no, I'm not. He gets his looks from you, but his brains from me."

"As long as he doesn't get your driving skills, he'll be fine."

Our family was now complete—I had my wife, my daughter, and now my son. Life couldn't be any better.